SUMMER'S DIRTY

LITTLE SECRET

ERNEST M

GOOD2GO PUBLISHING

SUMMER'S DIRTY LITTLE SECRET

Written by Ernest Morris

Cover Design. Davida Baldwin

Typesetter: Mychea

ISBN: 9781947340138

Copyright ©2017 Good2Go Publishing

Published 2017 by Good2Go Publishing

7311 W. Glass Lane • Laveen, AZ 85339

www.good2gopublishing.com

https://twitter com/good2gobooks

G2G@good2gopublishing.com

www.facebook.com/good2gopublishing

www.instagram.com/good2gopublishing

1

July 1996

***"Bitch, where you at! I'm gonna fuckin' kill yo' hoe ass!"* Nate** yelled as he busted through his front door with his Glock in his right hand.

Nathaniel "Big Nate" Barnes wasn't even a solid two months out of prison and here he was in his own living room, minutes away from doing something that might send his black ass right back. And probably for the rest of his life. He just finished a three-year sentence at Stateville Prison, right outside of Chicago, for drug trafficking. It was his first-time offense, and since he had no prior criminal history, he luckily copped a short sentence. Usually he was good with his runs, but a broken headlight on a foggy, raining day led to the discovery of a brick of coke in the back of his BMW. Big Nate was one of the biggest kingpins on the South Side of the Chi.

He pushed everything from coke and heroin to weed and pills. Although he was clicked up with a gang, Big Nate was a devoted family man and didn't like spending his time in the streets. All he

cared about was his money because money is what allowed him to take care of his family. Before he went to prison, Big Nate entrusted his best friend and day-one nigga, Quan, to take care of the business and his family. He was the godfather to Nate's daughters, Summer and Serena. Nate loved Quan like his own blood brother.

Hell, he was his brother. Before he went in to start his bid, without asking any questions, he knew he was doing the right thing by letting Quan take over in his absence. Shortly after Big Nate got out, everything seemed to return to normal—until one day someone, actually a few of his close people, started chirping in Big Nate's ears that Quan overstepped his boundaries. And not just with business, but even with Aisha. When niggas get to talkin' shit, gossip and innuendo have their way of spreading faster than AIDS in the streets. Apparently, Boone, one of Nate's hittas, told him he'd seen Quan and Aisha on several occasions sneak around and do some questionable shit. Nate at first didn't believe it and almost had Boone killed. But then Juice, another one of Nate's workers, suggested the same. Still with no verifiable proof or hardcore evidence, Nate took the word of his people and immediately decided to confront Aisha and then Quan.

Nate angrily stormed through his living room, ready to extract the truth. Once he cut the corner and made his way down the dark

hallway of his South Shore bungalow, he arrived at his bedroom door. He figured Aisha was in there hiding from him. He was drenched in his own salty sweat, so wet you would've thought he was outside all day long in the streets in the blazing summer sun. But it wasn't the sun that had Nate soaked in his own sweat, it was downing an entire bottle of Courvoisier and snorting two grams of raw Colombian white powder up his wide nostrils. His breathing was heavy and fast. His eyes were wide open, reddened, and glassy. The cocktail of alcohol and coke raced through his thick crimson blood a million miles an hour, making his heart a beat away from a massive stroke or heart attack. When he first got the news, a few of the guys earlier tried to get him to chill out and wait to do something until he had solid proof, but Nate refused. He got so damn high and drunk, his buddies tried to get him to calm down and sober up so he wouldn't end up passing the fuck out and dying. But his niggas' pleas fell on deaf ears because he felt as if he was already dead.

Hearing allegations of his wife's possible adultery and his best friend's betrayal made him feel like he had his heart ripped of out his muscular chest, shredded into thousands of pieces and fed to his pit bulls. All his logic was crushed up and thrown out the window of his BMW like an empty can of pop. He quickly tried to open the door, only to realize his wife had locked it. Now he

knew for certain her ass was inside. And she was—hiding behind their king-sized bed along with her two daughters, Summer and Serena, cuddled in her tight embrace, everyone confused, wondering what was going on. As Nate tried hard to break the doorknob with his grip, he kept viciously pounding on the door.

"OPEN UP THIS DOOR, BITCH! YOU AIN'T GON HIDE FROM ME!" he yelled, foaming at the mouth.

"Please, Nate, calm down! You're scaring Summer and Serena! Please! You're really high! Let's talk about this later when you're sober, baby! Just leave before I have to call 9-1-1!"Aisha begged.

Aisha along with her two girls were crying and visibly shaken by Nate's actions. Especially Summer and Serena. They didn't even have the slightest clue as to why their daddy was acting so strangely violent and menacing. To the girls, he was the complete opposite. Their superhero, their guardian, their protector. He did everything for them. But now here they were, hearing and seeing a completely different, unrecognizable, monstrous side of a man always packed with jokes, laughter, surprise gifts, and most importantly, relentless love.

"BITCH! SO NOW YOU THREATENING ME!" Nate twisted his chubby face up at hearing his adulterous wife threaten to call the boys in blue. She should've never done that though

because now his rage went from 10 to 1000.

BAM!

Nate, who was tall and at least a good 250 pounds, used his broad shoulders to explode his way through the bedroom door, breaking it off its hinges with ease. His eyes widened even more as they immediately attached to Aisha. He watched her and his girls in a frantic move deeper into the corner of the bedroom. Nate rushed around the bed and to the corner, and once he was inches away from Aisha, he leaned down, grabbed her with his left hand by her blouse collar, and snatched her off the ground and away from their sobbing and terrified daughters. Summer, twelve, the oldest daughter, still held on to her mother while her father tried to drag Aisha away to another side of the room.

"Daddy, please, no! What are you doing? Don't hurt Mommy! Please stop!"

"STAY YO' ASS OVER THERE!" Nate growled at Summer. His daughter's plea went through one ear and out the other.

For a split second, he took his heavy hand off Aisha and tried to tear Summer away from her. He brutally grabbed his daughter's arm, which was the first time he'd ever even put his hands on his daughter in such a manner, and then threw her hard down to the ground next to her sister, Serena, who was still huddled in the corner crying.

Nate's attention quickly turned back to Aisha. The fleeting moment she was free from Big Nate's grip, Aisha tried to get up and make a run for the door. Summer got up, lunged toward Nate and tried to tug his arm away from her mother.

"WHERE YOU THINK YOU GOIN'!" Nate growled with his finger on the gun's trigger. But then instantly became distracted by Summer's faint pull on his arm.

POW!

"AHHHHH! MOMMY!" Both Summer and Serena shouted in unison as they just witnessed their father shoot their mother in her back—by accident.

Aisha fell face forward to the floor, not too far away from the bedroom door. Nate quickly rushed over to his immobile wife. Seeing a river of blood flow from her back down to the floor to form a thick puddle quickly sobered him up. He truly didn't mean to shoot at his wife. He was aiming for the wall, but Summer's pull on his arm unfortunately threw the gun's aim right into the center of Aisha's back. Truth be told, Nate just wanted to scare Aisha to get answers, at least get her side of the story. Hell, he didn't even know if what was told to him was even true. In his coked up, delusional mind, he figured the gun would get her to quickly fess up. He leaned down and hovered over his wife, taking in the massive, smoky gunshot wound in the middle of her back.

"Baby, baby, baby, please, I'm sorry. Oh my God. I'm so sorry. I didn't . . . I didn't mean to shoot you! I swear," he cried as he dropped the gun, picked her up off the floor, and held her.

As Nate wept and rocked Aisha back and forth, her eyes were wide open, unblinking, looking directly into Nate's regretful, teary eyes. Her breathing was slow and shallow and she rapidly shivered with the fear taking over her body. As she tried to cough up some words, she choked up blood.

"I . . . I-I . . . didn't do it. I swear . . . I didn't do it. I love you, Nate . . ." she managed to mutter as tears trickled out of the corners of her angelic hazel eyes.

"Summer, go call the ambulance! Go!" Nate barked.

Suddenly Summer and Serena got up from the corner and dashed over to their parents. Both girls, ignoring their father, held on to their mother, crying, hoping she wouldn't slip away.

"Mommy! Please! Please don't die!" both daughters screamed and cried.

Nate, seeing how his oldest daughter didn't follow his command, grabbed Summer by her shirt.

"SUMMER! I SAID GO CALL THEM NOW!" he bawled and then pushed her away from her mother.

Summer lunged toward a beige landline phone sitting on a nightstand on the right side of the bed. She picked up and

immediately dialed 9-1-1.

"9-1-1, what's your emergency?" Nate could faintly hear the 9-1-1 operator's faint flat voice reverberate from the phone.

"Yes, my mother's been shot and she's dying! Please, someone send an ambulance quick!" Summer screeched into the phone, looking at her father hold her mother, who seemed to still be holding on to her life.

"Okay, calm down, ma'am. What's your address?" The 9-1-1 operator replied.

"312 South Indiana Avenue! Please send someone ASAP!"

"We will, ma'am. The police and the ambulance are coming now. Are you safe? Who shot your mother?" The 9-1-1 operator inquired. Summer paused for a moment and looked at her father.

"My father. He shot her." Her father suddenly looked up at his daughter and slowly shook his head no. Summer stared back at Nate as regret, fear, and grief swamped his face.

"Your father shot your mother?" The 9-1-1 operator wanted Summer to confirm what she'd just told her. She went silent. She seemed reluctant to admit her father just shot her mother.

"Yes!"

"Is he still there?"

"Yes, he is."

"Are you safe? Where is he?"

"Yes . . . Yes, I'm safe. He's in the room with me."

"Stay safe. We're sending someone ASAP."

Nate knew for sure now his life was over. He fucked up. Fucked up big time and nothing could undo the overwhelming trauma he just put his entire family through. He looked at Aisha. She was still breathing, trying her best to hold on.

"I'm sorry, baby, I'm so sorry," he plead as he continued to rock her back and forth in his arms. He was now covered in her blood and he could feel her limbs get cold.

"I know, I know," she muttered in pain.

"I love you," Nate squeaked.

"I love you too . . ." Aisha whispered and then fell silent.

Her shivering became motionless. Her eyes grew larger and her pupils began to dilate. Nate could feel his wife's breathing go silent and her body go stiff. He knew she was gone. He held her tighter, crumpled up his face as tears streamed down his face.

"No, no, please, baby, no, don't go."

Hearing her father say those words suddenly prompted Summer drop the phone and dash back to her mother. Both daughters clung to their mother's lifeless body, sobbing and hollering, asking God to bring her back. But Nate knew she wasn't ever going to come back. And he wasn't going to come back from this either. He wiped his face clear of sweat and tears and then

released Aisha from his embrace. He stood up, picked up his gun, and walked over to the corner of the room.

"I love y'all. Y'all know that, right?" Nate somberly asked.

Summer and Serena glanced over to their father, who now had the barrel of the gun up to his temple. He cocked the gun back. He tightened his face, closed his eyes. "Daddy, no, please!" Summer begged.

POW!

2

October 2006

Summer and Serena now found themselves not knowing what
their future was going to be. They were all they had in this fucked-
up, cold world. After their father murdered their mother and then
turned the gun on himself, the two girls had no one else to support
them or care for them. Neither of their parents had any siblings.
The few older distant cousins and family friends that knew the
girls didn't want anything to do with them due to their father's
notorious street reputation.

Besides, since Big Nate was dead now, his once overflowing
dope money well dried up like the Sahara Desert, and the distant
cousins and friends who were always there leeching off Big Nate's
wealth quickly turned unsympathetic towards the girls' situation
and went ghost. The State of Illinois quickly took custody of the
girls and put them into a temporary group home with other
orphaned children until they were either adopted by a kindhearted
foster family or perhaps some other unknown relative came and
claimed their lost kin.

~ ~ ~

Two months had passed since the death of their parents. One afternoon, after school, the two sisters got word they were going to be leaving the group home.

"Summer and Serena, I got some good news. We found you a foster family," Mrs. Johnson, the group home social worker informed the two girls in her office.

"For real?" Summer slowly asked with a raised doubtful brow.

"Who are they? Are they nice?" Serena quickly asked. She looked more excited about the news than Summer.

"Yes, of course they're nice! I told them about y'all too. Their names are Mr. and Mrs. Kaskowitz. They're coming this Saturday to pick y'all up too. They live in Winfield. Y'all been there?" Mrs. Johnson, the portly social worker, asked in her deep Southern accent.

"They sound white." Summer rolled her eyes and folded her arms.

"How are white people gonna raise black girls?" Summer asked with sarcasm laced in her question.

"Ahhh, Summer. White people adopt black children all the time. It doesn't matter if you're black, white, Spanish, Chinese, Arab, whatever. So long as they love y'all unconditionally, provide for you, care for you, and give y'all the support you need,

their color doesn't matter."

"I guess . . . we'll see." Summer still sounded doubtful, but honestly she dreaded the group home and would love to sleep in a regular, comfortable bed. Not the thin, pissy bunkbed mattress her and her sister were forced to sleep on here at the group home.

After Summer and Serena left the social worker's office, they now had to prepare for another abrupt change. But why couldn't the social worker find a loving black couple to adopt them, Summer wondered. Were there not any black couples out there who wanted to adopt two black girls? Saturday finally came. The girls had packed all their bags and were minutes away from meeting their new adoptive parents—the Kaskowitzes. After the girls said their goodbyes to some of the friends they managed to make at the group home, Mrs. Johnson, along with one of the security guards at the home, helped the two girls to the front lobby where the Kaskowitzes were patiently waiting to meet their two new daughters.

As Summer slowly walked down the hallway, she could see from afar the white couple standing there, smiling, as if they never had a single damn problem to go through in life. Although that seemed to be true off first glance, especially given Summer always thought white people had it a thousand times easier than black folks, it was far from true. John and Susan Kaskowitz were both

in their early fifties and had been married for nearly thirty years. Susan was diagnosed with uterine cancer in her twenties, and after years of chemotherapy treatments, her chances of getting pregnant shot to zero. After nine miscarriages and expensive fertility treatments, the barren couple finally decided to give up trying to have children on their own.

Mr. Kaskowitz was an affluent real estate attorney, working for the largest law firm in downtown Chicago. Mrs. Kaskowitz was an accomplished concert pianist and a professor at Scranton University in Lackawanna County. She also owned and managed a private music school. The couple previously adopted a baby girl from Nigeria. But unfortunately, after living with the Kaskowitzes for a year, the baby girl, Olufemi, passed away due to complications from AIDS. The baby girl's death was devastating to Susan, but a year after the baby's death, the couple decided to give adoption another try—this time with Summer and Serena.

"Mr. and Mrs. Kaskowitz, here they are: Summer and Serena Barnes!" Mrs. Johnson introduced the two girls.

Summer looked up at her new parents in disbelief and slight embarrassment. She couldn't wrap her mind around the idea of having some random-ass white folks be her new parents. Shit, she couldn't even fathom the idea of living in a part of Scranton she had never heard of before Mrs. Johnson told her. Mr. Kaskowitz

was short, had a head full of gray hair and a big hooked nose, and wore a yarmulke. Mrs. Kaskowitz was taller than John, voluptuously shaped, and had this intense red, curly hair matched with a face full of freckles.

"Oh my God, you two are so adorable! Cuter than your pictures! Come, give me a hug!" Susan cried the moment she saw Summer and Serena.

Without even asking, Mrs. Kaskowitz leaned down and passionately hugged the two girls as she landed kisses all over them. Summer kind of jumped back, alarmed that the white woman was so quick to kiss her, but Serena seemed to enjoy the newfound affection.

"Oh, I'm so sorry, baby doll. I've just been waiting for this day forever!"

Summer fake smiled. "It's okay, it's just gonna take me a minute to get used to all of this." Mr. Kaskowitz laughed and went to go shake Summer's hand.

"Summer, I'm John. You don't have to call me Dad, Daddy, Father, or any of that. I know this is gonna be an adjustment for you two girls, but listen, Susan and I are so happy to be here for you two. We aren't gonna impose on you. We just want the best for you two." Summer still looked unfazed and produced a slight anxious smile. Mr. Kaskowitz chuckled, sensing Summer's slight

nervousness.

"I understand you like comic books, Summer? I have the entire Marvel series all the way from 1969. You can check it out when we get home."

The second "comic books" slipped out of Mr. Kaskowitz's mouth, Summer glued her complete attention to him. He instantly won her over. The one thing she loved the most were comic books. Oddly enough, Big Nate, too, was a huge comic book fan, and it was the one oddly unique thing him and his eldest daughter had in common. Before he died, he used to always take Summer to First Aid Comics up in Hyde Park, and the two would spend hours going through different book collections. Summer's whole outlook on being adopted by some random white people was starting to change. Now she was willing to give the Kaskowitzes an opportunity to show her and her baby sister some sincere affection, something the two had been yearning desperately for now for months.

Once all the girls' bags and suitcases were packed in the back of Mrs. Kaskowitz's Land Rover, Mrs. Johnson said her goodbyes to Summer and Serena and wished them luck with their new family. Mr. Kaskowitz chucked up the luxury truck's engine and looked back at Summer and Serena.

"You girls heard that new Fugees album?" he asked with huge

grin on his face. "I love Lauryn Hill," he continued. Serena and Summer looked at each other with their mouths hung wide open, surprised that an old white man like Mr. Kaskowitz would even know about the Fugees.

"YES! Ohhh La La La! It's the way that we rock when we're doing our thang!" The girls sung in unison. Mrs. Kaskowitz turned around and smiled at the girls.

"Ohhh La La La La La La La Lalalah La Lah, sweeeeeeet thing!" The new happy family took off to Scranton.

Scranton was a far contrast from Philadelphia—shit, an even crazier contrast from the South Side where Summer hailed from. Although Big Nate took good care of his family, putting them up in a huge bungalow in South Shore, giving his wife and girls everything they ever wanted, South Shore wasn't necessarily the ideal place to raise a family. Summer grew up having her fair share of hearing gun shots, seeing an occasional dead body laid out in the streets, or seeing a harem of crack hoes parade up and down 79th Street, looking to suck dick for a high. Big Nate always used to tell Aisha one day he'd get out of the dope game and put his money into something legitimate like real estate, restaurants, or laundromats. Then eventually he was gonna move them out of South Shore and into a big-ass house with a big-ass front yard, back yard, inside pool, and jacuzzi somewhere out in the south

suburbs like Orland Park or Matteson.

While that never came true for the family, ironically, through Big Nate and Aisha's death, Summer and Serena now had a chance to experience just that. After driving up the expressway for over an hour and out of the city, Summer was instantly taken back by the massive palaces and mansions that lined Lake Shore Drive. Up to this point in her life, the biggest types of houses she'd ever seen were the mansions in Greenridge or in Colindale.

Those were big to her, and she always used to tell Big Nate when she got older, she was gonna own a house just like that. But the houses in Scranton? Summer was completely stunned people actually had the money to live in these houses, which seemed more like castles or the big luxurious mansions she would see TV stars live in when her mother would watch reruns of Lifestyles of the Rich and Famous. Mr. Kaskowitz finally pulled up to the black gate of his palace. Summer couldn't exactly make out just how big of a house she was about to live in, but if the surrounding mansions were any clue, she knew she was gonna be in for something beyond her imagination. After Mr. Kaskowitz rolled down his window and keyed in a security code, the massive black gate opened.

As he drove through, tall, well-manicured trees lined the roundabout leading to the house, still leaving Summer anxiously

curious as to what was going to suddenly appear. But seconds later, there the mansion was. Her mouth flung wide open at the sight of the massive gray-brick three-story mansion. Once parked, the two girls got out and walked up to the house, scanning everything around them. Summer was instantly taken aback by the fact that this massive fortress was now going to be her new home. She genuinely felt excited, but a part of her felt bittersweet knowing all of this came as a result of her dad murdering her mother then blowing his brains out in front of her and her sister. Two older Hispanic-looking housekeepers emerged from the double front wood doors of the house and scurried over to the truck, ready to move all the girls' suitcases and bags inside.

"Well, here it is, Summer. I hope you'll like it here," Mr. Kaskowitz said as he stood next to the still awe-stricken Summer.

"Yes! Thank you so much, Mr. Kaskowitz. Thank you!" she muttered as a tear of joy escaped the corner of her eye.

"You're welcome, Summer. And you don't have to call me Mr. Kaskowitz. You can call me John. I just hope one day you'll let me call you my daughter." He smiled.

After the girls got all their belongings inside and settled into their rooms, John and Susan gave the girls a tour of the immaculate mansion. It was exactly the very dream Big Nate always told Summer about when they would go on long car rides,

having their own special daddy-daughter bonding time. The Kaskowitz's didn't just have a front lawn; they had an entire estate. Their house sat on at least an acre of land, and nothing but greenery surrounded them.

The mansion had at least nine different bedrooms in addition to Susan's music studio and office, and an office and library where John kept his massive comic book and card collections. Right up Summer's alley. After the tour, the girls got down on a huge dinner made by the couple's personal chef. It was the first real meal the girls had in months. The chef, who just so happened to be a black woman, cooked a hearty dinner that made the girls feel right at home: oven-baked fried chicken, four-cheese macaroni and cheese, sautéed greens, sweet potato soufflé, and blueberry muffins. For dessert, the girls had strawberry cheesecake ice cream. Although the Kaskowitzes weren't too giddy about strict rules, they told the girls they usually went to bed around 11:00 p.m., but the girls could stay up and do whatever they wanted so long as they didn't do anything crazy. And honestly, John and Susan had nothing to really fear.

The girls, despite their situation, were raised to have very excellent manners and to always show utmost respect for people and their belongings. That's what Big Nate always taught them. Summer wanted to stay up to do more exploring of her own, but

between the long car ride, the overwhelming excitement, and the huge dinner, her body needed to crash. After she got Serena in bed, Summer took a long hot shower and put on a brand-new nightgown Susan gave her earlier as one of her many welcome gifts. She drifted herself to her new queen-sized bed filled with countless, plush pillows doused in a blend of calming lavender and eucalyptus essential oils. It was perfect aroma that led her to blissful, deep sleep. Something she hadn't experienced for a while.

"I love y'all. You all know that, right?" Nate somberly asked.

Summer glanced over to her father who now had the barrel of the gun up to his temple. He cocked the gun back. He tightened his face, closed his eyes.

"Daddy, no, please!" Summer begged.

POW!

The second Nate pulled the trigger a part of his skull exploded. Brain and blood splashed all over the place, some even sprinkling Summer's body. She dashed toward her father's seemingly lifeless body to see if possibly he was still alive. But he wasn't. Summer hovered over her father's body, blood oozing from his head.

"YOU'RE GONNA DIE TOO YOU FAST-ASS LITTLE BITCH!" Nate screamed as he swiftly stood up and then threw his

thick, bloody hands around Summer's throat, squeezing so hard, damn near snapping her trachea in half—GASP—with her heart pounding out of her tiny chest and sweat beads trickling down her narrow cappuccino face.

Summer woke up from her deep nightmare having a full-on panic attack. She jumped out of her bed and dashed to her bathroom. She quickly turned on the water faucet and splashed ice-cold water onto her face. She stared herself down in the mirror, trying her best to contain her rapid breathing and fast heart beats. But she couldn't. The more she tried to force herself to erase the vividly horrific image of Big Nate shooting himself, the more terrified she became, intensifying her panic attack. This wasn't the first time she had nightmares recounting that horrible day. However, this was the first time she dreamed of her suicidal father turning to a zombie with his head partly blown off and then trying to choke her to death. With tears racing down her cheeks, she tried her best to contain her cries so no one else would hear her. Perhaps drinking some lemonade or orange juice would help her, she thought, so she raced out of her bedroom and down to the kitchen to get something to drink.

Once downstairs and in the kitchen, she saw Susan sitting at the dining room table, flipping through a magazine as she sipped some red wine.

"What's wrong, Summer?" Susan asked once her eyes landed on the frantic, crying Summer.

"Oh, nothing. Nothing serious. I think I had an asthma attack," Summer lied.

"Asthma attack? You have asthma? I didn't see that in your medical history. Are you sure it's not something else?"

"I'm sure. I just . . . It's just. Nothing. You won't understand."

"Summer, come here, please. I wanna understand," Susan consoled Summer with her arms wide open. Summer didn't move. She just stood there and began to let out a long, deep wail.

"It's just, this is all too much. So fast. Everything. I just can't believe all of this."

Susan got up from her chair and quickly made her way to the emotionally fragile Summer. She slowly wrapped her arms around Summer and rocked her back and forth. She then slowly walked the two of them to the living room and sat down on the couch.

"What happened? You still think about what happened, huh?" Susan asked.

"Yes. I just miss them so much. I miss my mama. My daddy. I just don't know why he had to do that. Why? It's just not fair. It's all so messed up," Summer moaned with tears still escaping her red grieving eyes.

"I know, baby doll. I know. It's all fucked up. Oops, I mean

all so messed up," Susan quickly corrected herself.

For a second Summer laughed hearing Susan drop an f-bomb. She didn't want to break down like this in front of Susan and honestly now she felt so weak and embarrassed. She tried her best to slow her tears, but as she sniffed, she reminisced her mother's wide, enchanting white smile and hearing her father's silly giggles. She couldn't help but wail again.

"I just don't know who's gonna love us like they did."

"Awww, Summer. Don't say that," Susan cried. She lifted the young girl's chin, wiped her face free of tears, looked at her, and smiled.

"I'm gonna love you all. I'm gonna try my damn best. That's why we adopted you, because we wanna love you."

Hearing those words was just what Summer needed. She hugged Susan hard and buried her face into her chest, hoping God, time, and the Kaskowitzes would heal her wounds.

3

May 2007

Many months had passed. Summer and her sister were adjusting well to their new home and family. Although at times the girls found themselves having their moments, still missing their real parents, they were slowly beginning to fully embrace calling John and Susan "Dad" and "Mom." This was something John and Susan so desperately wanted from the very beginning. A dream come true to have children of their own call them that. Both the girls were attending school, fitting right in with no problems. Summer was very good at drawing and painting. So John, recognizing the girl's budding talent, showered her with art supplies so she could further explore and blossom into her craft. Serena was always musically inclined, so Susan started teaching her the piano, and she was learning so rapidly.

In fact, Serena was learning so fast, Susan considered taking Serena out of school and homeschooling her so she could spend more time studying the piano. Everything was going so well.

Truth be told, it was a blessing for John and Susan because Summer and Serena were extremely pleasant, respectful, courteous, and thankful for their newfound home and parents. Before John and Susan started the search to adopt children, so many of their friends, even some relatives, warned them not to adopt children from the US, especially black children, due to all the trauma that so many go through. Luckily, they didn't listen because Summer and Serena were proving everyone very wrong.

The school bus pulled up to the Kaskowitz estate.

"Have a nice day, Mr. Clayton," Summer said to the bus driver as she and Serena made their way off the school bus.

The two of them walked up to the gate of the estate as the school bus took off. Summer put in the security code, the gate opened, and the girls sauntered through. As they walked, Summer asked Serena how her day was and what new piece of music she was learning for her summer recital. As soon as they made it past the trees and to the front of the house, before they got to the front doors, Summer noticed two unrecognizable cars in the driveway: an old black Cadillac DeVille and a beige Chevy Impala. She'd never seen both cars before and assumed maybe they belonged to the housekeepers. A faded Giants bumper sticker was slapped on the back of the Cadillac.

Two of the tires were donuts with missing hub caps. The

Chevy Impala looked newer, and as Summer looked closely at the back tag, she saw the words "State of Delaware" etched into the plate. Summer still didn't pay any great attention to the cars, as she was too focused on wanting to tell her parents some great news.

"Mom! Dad! Guess what happened at school today?" Summer roared as she made her way into the living room, looking for Susan and John to tell them she'd won a statewide art contest.

One of her paintings was going to be on display in the state capitol in Springfield. As soon as Summer hit the corner and made her way into the seemingly quiet living room, she quickly noticed something strange was going on. Millions of butterflies invaded the pits of her tiny stomach as her brown eyes immediately recognized Mrs. Johnson, the social worker from the foster group home. What in the hell was her fat country ass doing here, Summer wondered. She was on the love seat with a bunch of paperwork in her hand. Seated on the couch was an older, big, hauntingly dark-skinned man in a pin-stripe maroon suit with matching gators on his feet. He had a shiny bald head, a thick black goatee, and these extremely vexing and jaundiced eyes. Next to him was a woman, perhaps the man's wife.

She had a head full of gray hair tied up into a bun. She had on a long, purple, polka-dot dress with rundown faded black pumps

on her swollen feet. She sat there on the couch, hands on her lap, looking quiet, docile, and unmoved. Summer could've sworn she recognized these people, but she didn't. She had absolutely no idea who they were. Susan and John were seated in two chairs in the middle. Sadness was engraved across their puffy faces as if they had been crying relentlessly for hours.

"Summer. Serena. Have a seat. We actually . . . have some news to share with you all," John exhaled, directing the girls to sit down on another couch facing everyone.

Summer and Serena took their book bags off and cast them off to the side of the couch and then sat down.

"What's going on?" Summer asked as her eyes bounced between everyone in the room.

"Hey, Summer and Serena. Y'all remember me? Mrs. Johnson from the group home?"

"Yes . . . Why are you here?" Summer quickly responded in a flat, uninspired tone.

"Well, I got some good news! These are your grandparents! Your mother's side. They're here to take you all back to Chicago! Meet Mr. Reverend Luther Gaines and his wife, Mary."

"What? I don't even know these people. We don't know these people. How are you gonna make us go live with some random people we don't even know? My mother never even brought us

around these people!" Summer protested.

She couldn't believe this was happening. Were these people fucking kidding, she thought as she became injected with a huge dose of rage and anxiety. Serena began to slowly cry at the sound of what Mrs. Johnson was saying. The stern-looking grandfather got up from his seat, walked over to Summer, and looked at her.

"You remind me of your mama with that rebellious mouth. We gon' work on that. Aren't we, Hattie Mae?"

"Yessum," the grandmother replied slavishly with her head tilted low, eyes fixed on the living room carpet as if she had to get the old man's permission to give any other human being eye contact.

"You can't do this to me, Mrs. Johnson. Mom, Dad. Please. They can't take us. You're our parents now."

John and Susan shook their heads negatively as they embraced each other and wept.

"I'm so sorry, Summer. We love you all, but the law unfortunately in Pennsylvania is very clear. Since we haven't had you all for a full year, your grandparents can petition to take you all back since your adoption hasn't yet been fully certified."

"What? What does that even mean? This is just too much! This is fucking bullshit!" Summer screamed, resisting the idea that these random-ass country-lookin' negroes were going to take her

out of what seemed to be paradise and back to God knows where. Summer's attitude was quickly shifting.

She found herself no longer being held back in completely verbalizing her sentiments. She was now unhinged, ready to defend her and her sister. She just finally got used to being with John and Susan, and now, less than a year later, she was being forced to quickly forget her new parents and go back to some people she didn't know were blood.

"Summer, please, don't say that," Mrs. Johnson interjected.

Reverend Gaines swiftly turned his attention to Mrs. Johnson.

"See, that's what happens when you get raised up by these rich white folk. And watch your mouth, young lady. You don't talk to your granddaddy like that."

"You ain't my granddaddy. Nigga, I don't know you! Fuck you and fuck that old dumb bitch over there," Summer viciously spat, tears of rage creeping out of her eyes. She was now ready to get up and go toe to toe with this dude despite him being at least three feet taller and two hundred pounds heavier.

The already overbearing grandfather leaned down into Summer's face and grinned. "You lucky I'm in someone else's house; otherwise, I woulda pulled my belt out on you and gave you somethin' real good. Now I dun had enough of this. You go get yo' clothes and be ready in twenty minutes," the grandfather

growled. He looked at Serena. "You too, now go get. I got work to do. Y'all holdin' me up."

"I ain't goin' nowhere. And Serena ain't goin' nowhere either, fuck nigga."

"I'm warnin' you, lil girl. Don't make me do somethin' you gon regret."

Hearing the war about to go down in their living room, John and Susan raced to break up the potential fight between the grandfather and Summer.

"Girls, please, follow me," Susan bellowed as she grabbed the girls and went upstairs.

John stood there, somewhat holding the grandfather back. Once upstairs, Summer saw a majority of their stuff was already packed and ready to go. How long did Susan and John know about this? she thought. Both Summer and Serena had so much stuff, and it would've taken some serious planning to get the girls' stuff packed so quickly.

"How long did you know about this, Mom?" Summer screeched as she sobbed.

"Sorry, baby doll. We found out last week. We didn't wanna say anything because John tried his best to file an injunction with the court stopping that man, but there was nothing we could do. We are still going to try to fight this, okay? You just gotta be

patient for the time being. Okay?"

"How could you though? You couldn't do anything else? Lie? Hide us? You said you were gonna be here for us to love us. This isn't love. This is hate. We don't know that asshole downstairs," Summer cried.

"Shhhh, please. It might take some time, but we're gonna fight for you all, okay?" Susan did her best to assure the girls, but Summer wasn't buying it.

"Fine, whatever. Please, do whatever it is. Please, Mom," Summer begged. Between Mrs. Johnson's car and Granddaddy Luther's car, as he wanted to be called, the girls managed to pack all their bags and suitcases to make their way back to Chicago.

"I'm gonna ride with Mrs. Johnson," Summer muttered as she made her way to the front passenger seat of Mrs. Johnson's Impala.

"That's fine," Granddaddy Luther beamed. "I'll just talk to little ole Ms. Serena here. Ain't that right, Ms. Serena?" he asked as he rubbed the younger sister's shoulder in a very odd, slightly inappropriate manner.

"No, she's gonna ride with us too," Summer retorted as she grabbed Serena away from the menacing, towering man.

"Fine. Y'all better be on yo' best behavior in that car. You understand me?"

Summer quickly scrunched her face up and rolled her eyes. "Whatever. Come on, Serena." Granddaddy Luther just shook his head side to side, looking disappointed. He pulled out a pack of Newports, slapped a square in his mouth, and lit it up.

"Hattie Mae, let's go 'fo these churren drive my nerves bad. Drive, woman." Summer and Serena for the last time, dashed toward John and Susan and hugged them tightly.

"We'll be in touch. We're gonna fight this thing for you guys, okay?" Susan cried with tears pouring out of her eyes. John tried to fight back his tears but eventually caved. Serena didn't want to let go, but Summer pulled her away.

"C'mon, sister. It'll be alright. We're coming back. These clowns aren't gonna have us for too long."

"I hope so, Summer," Serena cried as her and Summer jumped into Mrs. Johnson's car. Once out of the driveway, Summer looked through the side-view mirror, seeing John and Susan wave good-bye. Susan blew a kiss. Summer blew one back.

4

Was this all one big, crazy-ass, fucked-up nightmare Summer would soon wake up from? She desperately hoped so. The moment she left what was supposed to be her new family and now found herself with her new guardians—her actual "biological" grandparents—to her, everything was quickly sinking down into a deep abyss of violent quicksand. Everything was spiraling out of fucking control. As Mrs. Johnson followed Granddaddy Luther and Grandma Mary Hattie Mae to their apartment in Grand Boulevard Towers, Summer knew some serious fuck shit was about to become of her next new family. Grand Boulevard Towers, better known as "the Towers" in the streets, was one of Chicago's most notorious high-rise housing projects on the South Side. The Towers were a vast cesspool of every fucked-up thing about the Chi. Gangs. Drugs. Murder. Addiction. Prostitution. Joblessness. Fucked-up schools. All types of insane nigga madness went down in the Towers. As soon as the two-car entourage exited the expressway, they got onto King Drive and made their way to the massive multi-tower sore thumb on 39th Street. The second the dark gray towers became visible to

Summer, tears formed in the corner of her eyes.

"Mrs. Johnson, we can't just go back to the group home until all of this is sorted out? I mean, y'all sending us to live in the projects with people we don't even know. My mama told me she ran away from home from her parents. We never met them. This ain't right."

"Summer, just relax. You need to calm yo' behind down! That stunt you pulled back at Mr. and Mrs. Kaskowitz's house was unacceptable. And, no, you can't go back to the group home. That is a temporary housing shelter. You have family now. And if Mr. and Mrs. Kaskowitz really wanna adopt you all, they gotta make a deal with your grandparents. And trust me, even if they don't make a deal, you do not wanna go back into the custody of the state, because y'all would've ended up with crazy-ass family somewhere out in some trailer park in Indiana. Mr. and Mrs. Kaskowitz are rare people. Good people. Salt of the earth. But people like that don't often adopt children. Especially black children. Listen, I'll talk to your granddaddy about maybe allowing y'all to do split custody, but this is your new home. Deal with it."

Hearing Mrs. Johnson talk down to her as if she was completely naïve was pouring gasoline on a small and growing uncontrollable fire raging inside of Summer. She was three

months shy of her thirteenth birthday, and slowly but surely, she was becoming a young adult with a young adult attitude and mouth. The stress and trauma of trying to make sense and cope with her parents' death compounded with going from home to home was starting to make the young girl crack.

"Deal with it? DEAL WITH IT? The fuck you mean deal with it, huh? How the fuck would you like if you had to see your own father kill your mother, all over a damn rumor about her sleeping around?"

Serena in the back, visibly emotional herself, interrupted. "Please, Summer . . ."

"No, Serena, let her talk. She needs to let it out," Mrs. Johnson rebutted.

"ANSWER ME, BITCH!"

"Summer, I don't kn—" Before Mrs. Johnson could finisher her sentence Summer angrily interrupted.

"I KNOW YOU DON'T KNOW! How would you like it if you got bounced around, from one stranger's house to the next? How would you like it if you had to go live in the fucking hood? Granted, my daddy was a drug dealer, but he took good care of us and never in a million years did he have us living in no fucking bullshit like this. Look at all these fucking crackheads, hoes, and dope boys standing outside. What the fuck kind of help are you?

Come on, Serena. I'm done dealing with this fat country bitch."

Summer's teary, somewhat reddened eyes turned to slits. She opened the car door, got out, and made her way to the back of the trunk. Mrs. Johnson looked out the window into nowhere particular and exhaled deeply.

"Serena, I'm sorry about all of this. I truly am. But I am sure it's not gonna be that bad."

"Whatever," the little girl sassed as she opened the car door and got out. When Big Nate was still alive, he used to drive his daughters around here, not for pleasure or leisure, but to show them where he didn't want them to end up.

Ironically, Grand Boulevard was where he and Aisha were from. Where they actually met each other back as teenagers in the '80s. There was a time when Big Nate considered the Towers his stomping grounds and the base for his growing dope business. But after a series of shootouts he got into with a rival gang, on top of having a new wife and daughter, he decided to get the hell up out of Dodge and move to a safer area. That's when he bought his huge bungalow in South Shore, rehabbed it, and made it his own. His wife, Aisha, was the only child of Reverend Luther and Mary Hattie Mae Gaines. Luther and Mary were transplants from Mississippi who moved to Chicago in the late '60s when their daughter was still a baby. At the time when they moved here,

Grand Boulevard wasn't as dangerous as it is today, but Granddaddy Luther never left because he didn't' like the idea of paying for rent or a mortgage. He'd rather deal with rats, roaches, dope boys, pimps, hoes, and other types of vice in exchange for free rent. Granddaddy Luther was a preacher of a small, storefront Pentecostal church, Mt. Tabor Holiness Temple, about a block away from Grand Boulevard. He didn't have a big congregation, maybe only thirty members on a good day, and to support his household, he worked as an assembly worker at a Nabisco plant on the far southwest side of the city. Aisha never gave Summer too much information about her grandparents. All her mother ever told her is that she left home at an early age because her grandfather was too mean and partly crazy. And to make the situation even worse, when her and her father would get into fights, her mother, virtually powerless, did little to nothing to intervene. Once inside their building, Summer and her sister strolled behind Granddaddy Luther and Grandma Mary. Summer struggled taking in the desolation, ratchetness, and disgust of now her fourth home in less than a year. As she walked down the dimly lit hallway toward the elevators, she suddenly found herself overcome with deep nausea, not only since this was going to become her new wretched reality, but also because an overpowering smell of urine, malt liquor, cigarettes, fried chicken,

shit, and fishy pussy invaded her nostrils. This was the exact mélange of odors Big Nate always told her about. The unnerving deathly smell of entrenched poverty was like none other, and now Summer quickly realized why her father and mother had escaped this fucked up, disgusting place. Luckily, she didn't eat anything earlier; otherwise, she would've thrown the fuck up all over the place. Once Summer, her sister, and their grandparents made their way to the elevator, Summer noticed a severely underweight dark-brown-skinned woman off to the cut, singing and dancing as a small black radio next to her on the sticky ground blared Marvin Gaye's "Sexual Healing." The woman was obviously super high as shit, off in her own demented la la land, doing a two-step and snapping her long fingers.

She had on nothing but a light purple tank top riddled with holes and stained with brown spots. White crust covered the cracking corners of her ashy, red lipstick-painted lips. Half her head was shaved, and the other half had patches of unpermed hair. One patch was twisted off into a long braid with a purple barrette at the end. What drug or drugs was this bitch on? Summer speculated as she did her best not to gawk too hard.

"Oh hey, Rev.! Dem is yo' grandbabies you was tellin' me about?" The woman's dancing and raspy, off-beat singing came to an abrupt stop once her glassy bug eyes got a glare of the two

girls glowing with anxiety and disgust. She walked up to Summer and Serena, hands on her hips, smiling, exposing a mouth filled with a few of her remaining rotten teeth.

"Gimme a hug. I'm Loretta, yo' neighbor! Girl, you look just like yo' mama!" the crack hoe shouted directly toward Summer. She reached in and tried to give the girls a hug, but they resisted, especially the now-rebellious Summer.

"Bitch, get the fuck off me!" Summer cocked her fist back, ready to beat that crack hoe's emaciated ass.

"Ughh, what is yo' problem? You wanna fight me? C'mon then!" Loretta threw herself into a karate pose, waving her hands up and down as if she even stood a real chance of going up against Summer, who was obviously much healthier and twenty pounds heavier.

"No, no, no. Hey, y'all stop!" Granddaddy Luther hollered as he intervened and tugged the girls away from Loretta's attempted embrace.

"Sister Brown, leave them be. They've never been here before and this one right here is a bit feisty," said Granddaddy Luther, who kind of switched gears a bit and found himself defensive of his kin. He then rushed them along with Mary through the elevator.

"Here's two dollars. I'll see you later . . ."

"Okay, Rev.! It'll all good. Nice to meet y'all!" She waved goodbye as the elevator doors closed, and restarted her shuffle and singing to Earth, Wind & Fire's "Devotion." After a long, raggedy ride to the twenty-second floor, Summer and the rest of the clan arrived at apartment 2210. Granddaddy opened the thick maroon door and escorted everyone. The entire apartment wreaked of Pine-Sol, cigarettes, and bacon grease, a far contrast from the smell of lavender, eucalyptus, and chamomile at the Kaskowitz estate up in Winnetka.

"Well, here it is. Y'all's new home. Mary, go get supper ready so we can eat," Granddaddy commanded Grandma. Just like that Grandma Mary's quiet, docile ass zipped to the kitchen to go prepare dinner for everyone.

"I'ma show y'all ya new room. It ain't like what them white folks had. But it'll do."

Granddaddy Luther had the girls holed up in what was formerly their mother's old room. It was a tiny space with nothing but a twin-sized bed, a dresser, and a closet. Granddaddy went out and bought a small foldable mattress for Serena to sleep on. Complete fucking bullshit to Summer, given her and her sister just spent almost a year sleeping in their own rooms, on plush queen-sized mattresses covered in Egyptian cotton sheets.

KNOCK! KNOCK!

"Y'all . . . supper's ready, go wash up now!" Grandma Mary knocked on their bedroom and finally opened her mouth. The two sisters looked at each other in surprise and laughed. They never thought they'd hear that woman's voice.

"C'mon, let's go. This shit is crazy. We'll be out of here soon." Summer rolled her eyes and led her baby sister out of the room. Once the two girls got done washing their hands in what was now their bathroom, they made their way out to the dining room table where Granddaddy and Grandma were already sitting down waiting to eat.

"What took y'all so long? Y'all gon have my food cold. Next time, make it quick, or y'all ain't eatin'. Understand?" Granddaddy Luther barked as he puffed on a Newport.

"I guess . . ." Summer cut her eyes as she approached the table and pulled out her chair and sat down. Serena did the same.

"Lemme tell y'all somethin'. Y'all gon get right. All that disrespectful talk gon stop right now! Don't make me show you my other side. Here's the thing . . . When we get done, y'all gon wash the dishes, put on yo' pajamas, and come right out to the livin' room so we can do Bible study, and then y'all goin' straight to bed. Now bow ya heads so we can say grace," the menacing elder warned his granddaughters in his cracking dark voice, blowing thick Newport smoke out of his nostrils. He put his square

out in an ashtray overflowing with a mountain of hundreds of cigarette butts. Summer's eyes turned to slits. She didn't want to further agitate the old, stern nigga, so she just slowly shook her head and lowered it. From the moment she stepped foot into the apartment, she was planning her and her sister's escape. One way or another, she was gonna leave. It was just a matter of time. Granddaddy lowered his shiny bald head and clasped his thick, coarse, callus-filled ashy hands together over the table.

"Lord, bless this food we are about to receive and let it be nourishment for our bodies. In Jesus's name we pray . . . amen."

"Amen," everyone whispered. Summer didn't get a chance to look at the food before, but now she was paying full attention to what was on her plate.

Some nasty, slimy pink brownish meat mushed together with collard greens, black-eyed peas, and mashed potatoes. She loved collard greens and mashed potatoes, but black-eyed peas tasted like cat doo-doo to her.

"What's this?" Summer asked as she forked through her food.

"Good eatin', now eat up," Granddaddy replied, not caring about Summer's question.

"I just don't put anything in my mouth. So, I'm gonna ask again, and I am being kind. What in the hell is this?" Summer asked in her sassy voice.

Honestly, she had every right to ask because she'd be damned if she was gonna stuff some nasty-ass, undercooked meat down her throat and run the risk of getting food poisoning. Granddaddy suddenly dropped his fork and grabbed Summer by her shirt collar. "IT'S SQUIRREL! NOW EAT! I PAID GOOD MONEY FOR THAT GAME MEAT!"

"Get your fuckin' hands off me, nigga! I'm not eatin' that shit! You got me fuc—" SLAP! Summer flew out of her seat once Granddaddy Luther went across her face.

"Now I DUN TOLD YOU 'BOUT YO' MOUF!"

"No! Please, no!" Serena screamed at the sight of Granddaddy Luther getting out of his seat and hovering over Summer as she reeled in disbelief and pain.

But Summer wasn't gonna let the slap deter her from getting revenge. She got up off her feet and tried to throw punches at Granddaddy, but he was too strong, too overpowering for her to take him down. He grabbed Summer and dragged her down the hallway, slapping and punching her slender brown legs, arms, and even torso, trying to stop her from putting up any self-defense.

"See, you think I'm playin' wit ya! I got somethin' for that ass!"

Once he got down to an empty utility closet, he threw the door open and reached for a pair of handcuffs on a top shelf. Summer

was still kicking, punching, trying her hardest to get out of her evil grandfather's grip. Luther, unfazed by the girl's barely stinging strikes, used his thick, wide right hand to tighten his grasp around the girl's slim arm, damn near snapping it like a twig. Summer screamed out in pain and horror. Her grandfather was about to handcuff her to one of many pipes running against the wall in the closet. Once he cuffed her left wrist he slapped the other end of the cuffs to the pipe and took off his belt.

LASH! LASH!

"AHHHHH!" Summer screamed. This was the first time ever she'd experienced someone using severe physical punishment on her. Serena stood at the other end of the hallway screaming and hollering, begging Granddaddy to stop. Grandma Mary stood next to her side and consoled her and then walked her off to the living room as tears marched down her face. After a few more lashes from the belt, Summer caved in. The pain from the belt rendered her somewhat unconscious. She slowly slid down to the ground, cuffed to the pole. Granddaddy used his long thirteen-inch foot to kick Summer, shoving her further into the wide closet. He shut the door and turned off the light switch on the wall outside, imprisoning the girl to the dark, damp utility closet that wreaked of mold and mouse shit.

5

"You ready to behave yourself now, lil girl?" **Granddaddy** Luther growled as he creaked the utility closet door open and towered over Summer, casting his dark, deep shadow over her as she lay in a pool of her own urine, sweat, and fecal matter. It had been almost a week since Granddaddy Luther jailed Summer to the confines of the rancid utility closet. Her crime: a single charge of mouthing off. Her sentence: long, torturous days of being imprisoned in the dark closet without water, food, or the ability to use the bathroom to relieve herself.

"Ye-s . . . Yes . . ." Summer mumbled as she shivered.

Her now frail brown body was visibly pale, and she looked to be a good eight to ten pounds lighter.

"I can't hear you. You need to speak up in my house when I'm talkin' to you, lil girl. Are you gon act right?" Granddaddy muttered with a square dangling from his long, plump purple lips, a glass of chilled cognac in his hand.

As he awaited her reply, he took a sip of his liquor and swiveled the cognac around his gums as if it were mouthwash. He took a puff from his square, leaned down, and blew thick smoke

into the girl's sunken in face.

"I think you need another day in here," he threatened as he stood up, ready to slam the door shut on the battered girl.

"Yes, Granddaddy, I'll . . . be . . . on . . . my . . . bes-sst behavior," Summer murmured through her dry, dehydrated mouth.

She was extremely loopy. Everything around her was wobbling and spinning. She knew if she didn't get reprieve from her punishment, she was hours, shit, possibly minutes away from slipping into death.

"Good," Granddaddy snickered. "Mary Hattie Mae Gaines! Come get this young, impudent hussy and clean her up. We gon get da Jezebel out her," Granddaddy sternly assured as he uncuffed the girl.

"Yessum," Grandma Mary quickly scurried over to the utility closet.

"When you get done bathin' her, bring her to the dinner table for supper. We still got yo' plate of stewed squirrel," Granddaddy hissed.

"Yessum . . ." Granddaddy moved out of Grandma's way as the older woman helped Summer off the foul, sticky closet ground.

Once up, Grandma ushered a limping Summer to the

bathroom and gave her a good Epsom salt bath and helped her slip into a nightgown.

"Bow ya heads," Granddaddy mumbled in his cracking murky voice.

As usual, he lowered his head and clutched his hands together over the table. Everyone else followed suit, even Summer.

"Lord, bless this food we are about to receive and let it be nourishment for our bodies. In Jesus's name, we pray, amen."

"Amen," everyone whispered.

This was the first time Serena had seen her older sister in a week. She was thrilled yet nervous for her because it was very obvious she didn't look the same. Serena leaned into Summer's side, "You okay?" Serena whispered in her innocent voice as a faint cry almost escaped.

Summer turned to Serena and nervously smiled, "Yes, I'm okay."

Granddaddy suddenly pounded his heavy fist against the rickety mahogany wooden dining room table. Summer's and her sister's body trembled at the sound of the thunderous pound.

"Enough talkin'!" Granddaddy yelled. "Serena, eat ya supper. Summer, that squirrel ain't goin' nowhere. Ya betta eat!"

"Yessir, Granddaddy Luther . . ." Serena answered and began to fork through her food—pig's feet, lima beans, candied yams,

and corn bread.

Summer picked up her fork and mindlessly picked through the food. She stared down at the white ceramic plate and could see her reflection beam into her eyes. This was not a nightmare anymore to her. This was indeed her life, and she was not going to wake the fuck up from this, she thought.

"Put some hot sauce and vinegar on it. That's how I eat mines," Granddaddy said as he chowed down on his pig's feet.

Summer's eyes glanced over at a steak knife next to Granddaddy's plate. She imagined suddenly grabbing the knife and slicing the man's neck from ear to ear and then stabbing him to death. For a split second, she gave it contemplation and she felt the impulse to move her hand, snatch the knife, and hack her oppressor to death.

"Can I have some more lemonade, please?" Serena kindly asked.

Once Summer heard her sister's calm, guiltless voice she instantly snapped out of her bloody, murderous fantasy. She gawked down at the lukewarm, week-old, brownish pink, gelatinous squirrel meat on her plate. She knew if she tried to make that move, Granddaddy might be able to fight back and stop her. Then she wondered what would happen next. Granddaddy could, shit, would kill her, and then she would never ever see her

sister again. And then only God knew, if she did die, what kind of impact would that have on Serena? Would she still have to stay with their backward-ass grandparents in the projects? Would her grandfather then move to fuck with Serena? Summer didn't want any more unnecessary tragedy to befall Serena, so she quickly determined the risk of murdering her grandfather wasn't worth it. She picked up the hot sauce bottle, doused her squirrel meat, and began to chip away at the tree rat, numbing her mind to the gritty, off taste every time a chunk of the meat landed on her tongue and went down her throat.

"See, I told you it ain't that bad. Now finish up," Granddaddy commanded as he sucked on a pig's foot bone, juices and hot sauce plastered all over his lips and the corners of his mouth.

And so it was, Summer was slowly and surely beginning to learn how to be a respectful, "obedient" girl, abiding by all of the rules and laws of Granddaddy Luther's house. The girls had to acquiesce to this unfortunate, grim situation and hope their other "parents," John and Susan Kaskowitz, would rescue them and bring them back to what they truly considered home—far away from this ghetto-ass hell in apartment 2210. By the weekend, Summer and her sister had to learn and adapt to their new routine Granddaddy laid out for them. The girls were going to be starting up school again come Monday, and Granddaddy Luther wanted

them to transition with ease so he wouldn't have any problems out of them. Granddaddy set out an extremely strict and aggressive schedule of how their lives were supposed to go. Monday through Friday, Granddaddy expected the girls to wake up promptly at 4:45 a.m. to pray, eat breakfast, and then get ready for school. From 7:00 a.m. to 3:00 p.m., the girls were to be on their best behavior while in class. Any reports of bad behavior or bringing home unacceptable grades would amount to an automatic belt beating and confinement to their room. Immediately after school, the girls were to come straight home and do their homework since Granddaddy had an activity planned for them every weekday evening. Monday nights the girls had to help their grandfather clean the church. Tuesday nights were reserved for choir rehearsal. Wednesday nights were for Bible study. Thursday nights were slated for the girls to learn how to sew and crochet. Fridays were for revival. Saturdays all household chores and grocery shopping were to be completed. Sundays, the girls were going to be in church from 5:00 a.m. to 3:00 p.m. Afterward, the girls and their grandparents would eat a big Sunday meal, Granddaddy's favorite: stewed chitlins.

In fact, Summer spent her entire Saturday learning how to thoroughly clean and prepare chitlins the right way. The way Granddaddy preferred—slow cooked in vinegar, bell pepper,

onion, garlic, and other Southern seasonings, reminding Granddaddy of his Melba, Mississippi, upbringing. Grandma Mary taught Summer the best way to squeeze out all the tiny, hidden shit pebbles buried in the folds of the pink pig intestines. Then she taught her how to cut off all the extra fat and membrane. This wasn't exactly a great bonding experience between the grandmother and her granddaughter either since Mary Hattie Mae didn't really say anything other than just give simple, whispered instructions. Sunday evening arrived, and Summer and Serena were in bed already by 8:00 p.m.

After downing a big, copious bowl of hog guts served on a bed of white rice downed with a big, tall glass of red Kool-Aid, Summer said a prayer, crying to God, hoping her and her sister would soon be liberated from this newfound horrific fuckery. "God, are you listening?" Summer asked in her prayerful mind. "Deliver us," she begged as she could still feel remnants of chitlin slime coat the roof of her mouth. She cried herself to sleep, eager that going to school and making new friends would gift her restless, fearful, anxious mind a sense of peace.

6

Summer sat off in the far corner of a muggy classroom. She tried her best to get used to the strong aroma of chalk, mildew, old books, and a janitor's half-assed attempt to use watered down, off-label cleaning solution to cover up the thick stale smell.

The second she strolled through the door of the class, Summer instantly found the smell cantankerous, sneezing uncontrollably for a good minute. Her teacher's continuous spraying of cheap Elizabeth Taylor's White Diamonds perfume all over her wrinkled neck and cleavage didn't offer Summer relief either.

After getting adjusted to the stench of the old classroom, Summer sat silent, patiently waiting for her first-period eighth-grade English class to begin.

Today was her and her sister's first day back in school after leaving John and Susan, and truth be told she wasn't quite thrilled. Marcus Garvey Middle School was a far cry from the upscale, predominantly white Crow Island Middle School she attended

while she lived with the Kaskowitzes. Marcus Garvey was about a good four-block walk south of the Towers and maintained a notorious reputation for being not one of, but the worst middle school in the entire city. All the kids who attended were black, poor, and came from dysfunctional-ass families who either lived in the Towers or in low-income, Section 8 apartments scattered throughout the surrounding neighborhood.

Now, granted, before Summer's parents died, she went to a predominantly black school when she lived in South Shore. But most of those kids at Loomis Elementary came from relatively stable, working-class, two-parent households. Most of the kids at Marcus Garvey were either raised by an old, out-of-touch grandparent; a struggling single (possibly drug addicted) mother; a money-hungry, abusive foster parent looking for a quick, easy come-up; or possibly some sort of insane combination of the above. Looking to pass time until class began, Summer skimmed through the torn, graffiti scribbled pages of her used English textbook. It was crazy to Summer the school didn't replace these books. When she first opened the book and looked at who previously used it, she was shocked to see the first student to use it was a kid from the '70s. Other than the teacher, Mrs. Washington, who seemed so preoccupied with trying to solve the daily crossword puzzle in her copy of today's newspaper, only

about a good five or six students were in the class, including Summer. And the few who were in there had their heads on their desks, sleeping until the final bell rang. However, one young nigga in particular sitting to Summer's side had his shady bug eyes glued to her slender, growing body the moment she walked into the classroom.

"Aye, what yo' name is, lil shawty?" the young nigga, who to Summer looked way too old to be in her class, asked with a huge grin plastered across his ashy face.

He slowly raised his left hand and tickled Summer's shoulder, trying to get her attention. The second she felt his rough cold fingers land on her right shoulder, she quickly jumped back, screwed her face up, and slapped the young dude's hand off her shoulder.

"Don't touch me," she spat. "Get the hell away from me."

"Ahhh, c'mon, don't do me like that. I'm tryin' to be ya friend. You all new and shit," the young nigga attempted give his best shot at wooing his new sexy classmate.

Summer wasn't falling for his advances though. She rolled her eyes and tried her best to ignore him as she continued to anxiously skim through the frayed textbook. The aggressive and annoying young nigga licked his lips and smiled. In a sneaking manner, he reached down and tried to creep his long, dark, semi-ashy fingers

in between Summer's legs

"Man, lil mama, you thicker than a snicker, on God. You know I eat pussy, right? You like to get ya pussy ate? I'll eat that shit, on my mama's grave." The second Summer's eyes saw the young nigga's hands make its way to her inner thighs, she punched him hard in his shoulder twice.

"I SAID DON'T FUCKIN' TOUCH ME!" she growled as she got up and moved to a different seat.

Buddy smacked his teeth. "Well, fuck you too then, you ole busted down boujee bitch!"

7:57 a.m.

Scores of kids trickled into the classroom, loudly chirping away, making their way to their seats. A big, tall, overbearing, dark-skinned girl with a head full of dry, flaky finger waves approached Summer. Without hesitation, the stocky girl violently shook Summer's desk.

"UMMM . . . 'Scuse me, Ms. New Skinny Red Bitch, you need to get up! This my seat. Take yo' red ass elsewhere!"

Summer, looking confused and a tad nervous, closed her textbook. "Well, Mrs. Washington said there is no assigned seating, and that guy over there is bothering me," she murmured as she fiddled with a pencil on her desk.

"SKINNY RED BITCH! I don't care. You probably wanna

suck his lil dick anyways! NOW MOVE!" the unfazed, big black girl shouted.

Mrs. Washington was only inches away and observed the entire squabble. "KEISHA JENKINS! Leave that girl alone!" Mrs. Washington spat as she got up from her seat and gently slapped Keisha on her thick back with her now rolled-up newspaper.

"And what I told you 'bout yo' mouth?" Mrs. Washington was about a good sixty years old.

When Summer first introduced herself, Mrs. Washington was extremely upfront, making it known to her she didn't give two shits about her job anymore. So long as you came in at a decent time, didn't get into a fight, and turned in an assignment here and there, you were on good terms with her.

"Nah, Mrs. Washington, this lil ass girl gon sit in my seat! You know I like this seat!" Keisha bellowed.

Mrs. Washington just wanted Keisha's big ass to shut the hell up so she could get class started and go back to the crossword puzzle. Unsympathetic to Summer, the grumpy teacher said to her, "Summer, go sit over there by Zayn."

She pointed to a kid on the opposite side of the classroom.

"Yeah, go sit yo boujee red ass over next to that weird-ass AIDS crack-baby fag!" Keisha shouted as she let out deep, whale-

like, long chuckles.

Suddenly the entire class erupted in laughter.

"YO MAMA ON DAT CRACK ROCK! BOOM! BOOM-BOOM!" Some kids loudly sung in unison, mocking Zayn.

"HEY! HEY! HEY!" Mrs. Washington shouted. "Cut that shit out! Da hell is wrong wit y'all? I know y'all ain't talkin'! Half y'all mamas smoke crack! ANNNNDDDD, do other shit at THAT!" Mrs. Washington then looked down at Summer and tapped her desk. "Ms. Summer, come on. Get up and just go over there so I can get my damn class started."

It wasn't even 8:00 a.m., and Summer's nerves were already shot to the bottomless pits of hell. As she quickly stuffed her purple JanSport bookbag and got up, Mrs. Washington continued to rant as she sauntered her carefree big ass back to her. "I ain't got time for this bullshit today! Today is October 27, 1997. You know that means? It means I got 220 days, seven hours and a long-ass minute left to deal with you crazy-ass, no-good nigga churren! Now shut the hell up and read Chapter 20 for the next hour! And I don't wanna hear a GOD DAMN thang! Y'all understand me?"

"Yes ma'am . . ." everyone lowly muttered.

Summer was so blown back by hearing Mrs. Washington loudly curse left and right without a single care in the world. Although Summer cursed herself and obviously knew it was

normal for people to drop expletives left and right, she just didn't expect to hear it come from an old black teacher in a classroom with students present. She'd only been at school now for less than an hour and already was getting a feel for the daily chaos she might have to adapt to if she inevitably had to stay here and survive. She quickly got up and made her way to an empty seat near Zayn. As Summer got closer and closer to Zayn, she noticed Zayn didn't look as rugged and menacing as a good chunk of the other guys in the class. He was quite the opposite. He looked tall sitting down, a tad skinny, and wore glasses. Summer quickly glanced him up and down, quickly noticing he wasn't rocking the expensive designer clothes and Jordans the rest of the guys were wearing. His entire outfit looked like donated, hand-me-down clothes from the Salvation Army. Summer sat down, still gawking at him, as he didn't seem bothered by her sitting next to him. Summer knew kids loved throwing gossip out about people's parents being on dope or having AIDS, so she didn't really take what Keisha said moments ago seriously. But then as she got herself situated, she wondered if there was really something wrong with him. Was he autistic? Retarded? Deaf? He didn't look like he had a serious mental or physical handicap. But then Keisha did also call him a fag, so Summer speculated the possibility of Zayn being gay. Suddenly, Summer remembered a nugget of

wisdom her father, Big Nate, always used to tell her" "Never judge a book by its cover."

After sitting down and nestling her bookbag to her side, she couldn't help but notice Zayn write away in a black and white composition notebook. RING! RING! The final 8:00 a.m. school bell rang. After the school's principal got on the intercom, said the pledge of allegiance, and went over some school-related news, Mrs. Washington quickly reminded everyone in the class to get their asses to work by diving right into Chapter 20 of their textbook. The school was on a block schedule, which meant instead of students having to go to seven or eight classes a day, they would only go to three classes a day, each about a good two hours long. About a good thirty minutes into class, Summer noticed Zayn rip a piece of paper out from out of his composition book and slide it to her. Nervous he was trying to hit on her as well, she was reluctant to open it. What in the hell did he write her, she thought. She couldn't resist anymore, so she grabbed the letter from off the corner of her seat table and opened it up:

The power of a gun can kill, and the power of fire can burn. The power of wind can chill, and the power of mind can learn. The power of anger can raise inside until it tears you apart. But the power of a smile, especially yours, can heal a frozen heart—2Pac.

I just wanted to let you know don't be afraid to smile. I'm not

on that BS like the rest of these clowns. I stay to myself. I'm Zayn Hakeem. Nice to meet you. Sorry if I bothered you.

Summer's anxiety cooled; truth be told, she began to feel warm inside. Zayn simply introduced himself to her with a poem written by one of her favorite hip-hop artists, 2Pac, and she instantly felt a connection to the mysterious and somewhat eccentric classmate to the right of her.

She took out her pen and wrote him back: "That was so sweet. Thank u. I will try to smile. I am still trying to get used to all of this. I'm Summer Barnes. Nice to meet you, Mr. Zayn Hakeem." She smiled, folded the paper, and slid it back to Zayn. He opened it up, read her note, and then looked at her and smiled. He wrote back and then slid the note back to her. She grabbed it, opened it, and read it.

"We'll talk later. Let's not get in trouble. Mrs. Washington is somethin' else. Nice to meet you once again." She grinned once more, feeling somewhat excited perhaps she found a new friend she could talk to despite being in an environment filled with so much chaos and uncertainty.

She went back to reading Chapter 20, blazing through the chapter like a Dr. Seuss book. Summer was far too advanced for this class and truthfully should've been enrolled in an honors program. But she didn't mind though since she thought she now

had a leg up on everyone and would be able to make easy As. After class was dismissed, Summer went on to her other classes. She met a few other people here and there. But no one really piqued her interest like Zayn.

7

Many months had passed. For Summer and her sister, the bittersweet reality was surely sinking in: their fate was set. Granddaddy Luther and Grandma Mary Hattie Mae were now their new guardians. Many nights the girls, especially Summer, would cry themselves to sleep. Summer couldn't fathom how she would now have to spend the next four-and-a-half years of her life being reared by an overbearing, stern, oppressive man who she didn't know nor trust along with his submissive, docile wife. Summer felt so let down, even lied to, because she swore eventually the Kaskowitzes would come and rescue her and her sister and take them back home. But as each day passed, that seemed like it wasn't likely to happen. They girls didn't receive a single phone call, letter, or even visit. It was if as John and Susan totally forgot about them, or worse, never met them.

Summer and her sister loved the holidays, and this year was extremely hard because just last year they had the opportunity to be with two parents who showered them with so many gifts, so

much attention, and most importantly, tons of affection any young girl needed. This past Thanksgiving didn't feel special at all. Grandma Mary Hattie Mae and Summer whipped up a larger-than-normal yet simple dinner for the day. After quickly eating, Granddaddy took the girls to a local church to volunteer at a food bank and pass out dinners to the homeless.

Now Summer didn't mind helping the less fortunate, necessarily. Big Nate always told her, "To whom much is given, much is expected." She loved helping people, especially those down on their luck. But Summer felt she was down on her luck now and wanted someone to come help her. She just wished God would miraculously bequeath her one more chance to go back in time and relive seeing her mother's glowing face and smile as she taught her how to perfect making a Thanksgiving turkey. She yearned to go back and see her father stuff his chubby, affectionate face with all the good food her and her mother would make. She missed being at the dinner table with them, talking, enjoying their food, enjoying each other's company. Shit, enjoying their lives.

Hell, even Thanksgiving with the Kaskowitzes was a million times better than Granddaddy Luther and Grandma Mary's dry and uneventful bullshit dinner. Last Thanksgiving, John and Susan hosted a huge early afternoon party and introduced the girls to all their friends and family. Later that day, Susan took the girls

downtown to the Thanksgiving Day parade and then on a huge shopping spree. Now you know if this Thanksgiving with Granddaddy and Grandma was fucked up, then Christmas was even more depressing. Granddaddy Luther was a Grinch on steroids. He didn't believe in Christmas; in fact, he told the girls Jesus wasn't even born on December 25. To him, good Christians didn't exchange gifts or put up decorated trees because it was idolatry and blasphemy. Ironically, when Christmas day came, Granddaddy made the girls attend church all day long and then "gifted" them with a big bowl of souse soup—pig tails, pig ears, and hog maws—followed up with a scoop of some butter pecan ice cream. For Summer though, despite the mounting odds she faced, she was determined to make it out.

Everyday she'd spend hours thinking of how she would eventually make her way out of Granddaddy's virtual prison, out the craziness of the projects and to her own place so she could take care of herself and Serena, eventually getting their lives back on track. She had so many ideas. Her first and most realistic option was to go to college far, far, far away in a different state. That was why she wanted to make sure she kept on top of her education. She knew when she got to high school, she needed to work her ass off, make straight As and do everything in her power to get as much scholarship money as possible. With all the bullshit Summer

went through, she now wanted to become a family lawyer and stop bullshit like this from happening to other kids. But if for some odd reason or another that plan failed, her next option was to join either the air force or navy, serve her time, and then get the military to pay for undergraduate and law school education. Either way, she was getting the hell up out of this bullshit for good.

But for now, Summer made it her goal just to respect all of Granddaddy Luther's rules, do everything he required, no questions asked, and just bide her time. And it was working, at least for right now. Granddaddy hadn't put his hands on Summer since that first week.

At 2:21 a.m. Summer woke up from her sleep needing to use the bathroom to pee. She got up out of her bed and slowly strolled to her bedroom door. Once she creaked the door open, she heard keys jangle through the front apartment door. What the hell? she thought. Who in the hell was that? Then it hit her. Obviously it had to be Granddaddy Luther. He would be the only one up at this time in the morning doing whatever the hell he felt like doing.

Grandma Mary usually went to bed around 9:00 p.m., promptly after evening Bible study and prayer. Granddaddy would often stay up late at night, to either read his Bible or smoke cigarettes and sip cognac as he watched reruns of Sanford and Son. Summer stood by her door, silent, doing her best to figure

out what exactly Granddaddy was doing up this late or rather early in the morning. Truth be told, he should've had his old ass in bed because he had to be to work in a few hours.

"Ooooh, baby, I hope you got that good shit for me!" a raspy voiced echoed down the hallway.

Who in the fuck was that? "Shhhh, be quiet. You gon wake everyone the hell up. Go over there." Summer immediately recognized Granddaddy's dark, lowered voice as he was directing someone through the living room.

Summer quickly closed the door and dashed back to her bed. She wasn't going to run the risk of having Granddaddy hear her snooping. God knows if he caught her what type of ass whooping or other crazy-ass punishment he would subject her to. As she covered herself in her blanket, she couldn't resist the urge though to snoop. Who in the fuck was that voice? she wondered as she slowly slid the sheets off her body again once again and proceeded to get up out of the bed and to the door.

She slow creaked the bedroom door open, and like a ninja, slowly squeezed her slender frame through the narrow slit. She tip-toed down the hallway to the corner dividing the living room and kitchen. Once she found a safe spot, she ducked down and carefully listened. Then Summer heard the unbuckling and pulling down of pants and followed by the sound of someone heavy drop

to the couch.

"Damn, baby, you hard as a rock already. You miss this juicy pussy, huh?" the raspy female voice whispered.

As Summer's eyes widened in disbelief, she tried her best to figure out the voice. She knew she recognized it, but she couldn't quite match the voice with a face.

"Ahhhhh yeah, right there. Up and down, just like that. Go all the way down on it," Granddaddy Luther moaned as Summer also heard consistent slurping sounds go along with his blissful groans.

"Ah, ah, ah, slow it down," Granddaddy screeched. "You gon make me cum too fast. You know I like it slow."

"Sorry, Rev. I just love suckin' yo' dick. You got the biggest dick I ever seen befo'!" LORETTA! The voice finally hit Summer.

The fucking zombie-looking crack hoe! Summer was in complete shock and dismay her so-called holier than though, strict, preacher grandfather was in his own living room, getting sucked up by a half-dead, drug addicted prostitute at 2:00 a.m. A million thoughts flooded her mind as she continued to listen to her grandfather enjoy getting his old black dick slurped on by a woman who only had about a good three or four rotting teeth left in her loose gums. And then what about Grandma Mary? Summer thought, still surprised that this was even happening as

68

Granddaddy Luther's groans flooded her ears. How could he go and cheat on her grandmother like this? And how in the hell could he be so brazen and do this right in the living room. Summer instantly felt nauseated. She wanted to run to the bathroom and throw up her stewed rabbit dinner all over the place. But she managed to gulp and push down the rising acidic stomach chunks so she could persist in listening. She had to since there was one lingering question still unresolved. What in the hell did Loretta mean by "good stuff"? All of sudden the slurps stopped.

"You want some pussy too?" Loretta whispered.

"What da hell you think? Turn yo' narrow ass over," Granddaddy seductively barked.

"Good, 'cuz I've been waiting for a week to bounce on this dick."

"I know . . . And I'm gon tear through you like a slab of Memphis baby back ribs."

"Shit, I love it when you talk nasty to me, Rev."

After a few seconds of listening to the rumbling on the couch, Summer peeked her head around the corner. Luckily Granddaddy's back was facing her so she now had a good visual of what was about to happen. Granddaddy was standing up with his shirt still on, but his pants down, his big saggy brown ass exposed to her nosey eyes. Summer quickly covered her mouth

and squinted her eyes. Granddaddy's wrinkled ass wasn't the sight she wanted to see. But then she slowly opened her doe eyes back up and saw the reverend slide into Loretta and let out a deep moan.

"Throw that pussy back on me, bitch," Granddaddy bellowed as he gripped Loretta's frail shoulders and began to pound furiously inside the prostitute's pink middle.

Granddaddy better be careful, Summer thought, because Loretta looked like she weighed less than a plank of plywood. The two were going at it like caged monkeys in the zoo. Granddaddy was grinding and digging hard into Loretta, enjoying every second of her cracked-out pussy. With each pump, he'd let out a grunt as she also panted in enjoyment. By this point, Summer truly had seen enough. She quickly yet quietly stood up and tip-toed back down the hallway to her room. Once she squeezed through her door, she stood behind it, patiently and quietly waiting for Granddaddy's fuck session to come to an end.

"Ahhhhhhh! Shit! Shit!" Granddaddy barked.

This time he was a bit louder and Summer wondered if his screech would wake up Grandma. Or maybe Serena. Summer quickly looked at her sister as she slept away on the cot. Serena didn't flinch. She turned her eyes back to the door and continued to listen.

"Damn, you musta taken yo' fish oil or somethin', 'cuz yo'

pussy was so damn wet, I almost slipped! I oughta sue yo' ass, but you ain't got no money." Granddaddy laughed as Summer could hear him pull his pants and zip up his zipper.

Summer tightly held her mouth because now truth be told she really wanted to bust out laughing.

"Hahaha, you always got jokes. But, damn, Rev., you got me to'e up! I'm gonna need to soak in some Epsom salt."

"Okay, bitch, shut up and put yo' clothes on. Hurry up. I got work in a few hours. Here's yo' shit."

"Damn! Why you gotta be so mean sometimes. Anyways, I'ma smoke this and see what this hittin' on. I'll let you know if it's a good high."

"Yeah, good. Let me know, 'cuz that shit 'bout to hit the block in a few days."

And there it was—Granddaddy Luther was getting crack hoe head and pussy in exchange for a bag of rocks. This old nigga wasn't just a reverend, preaching salvation and hope. Granddaddy was out in the streets, selling dope. He was using Loretta to test out new product for the streets. Summer's stomach turned upside down at what she just heard. She raced back to her bed and jumped in. Although she still needed to pee really bad, she waited until the coast was clear. She covered herself in her blanket, wondering what in the fuck was really going on. Granddaddy Luther—a

fucking drug dealer. But then she wondered, was this the smoking gun she needed in order to get out of Granddaddy's grip?

8

"Terrell Bailey . . ."

"Here . . ."

"Summer Barnes . . ."

"Here . . ."

Summer raised her hand once she heard Coach Jackson, her PE teacher, call her name on his attendance roster.

"SKINNY RED BITCH!" Keisha shouted.

Everyone in the school gymnasium started laughing.

"HEY! HEY! SHUT THE HELL UP! AIN'T NO GOD DAMN CUSSIN' IN MY CLASS!" Suddenly everyone became quiet and motionless.

"What's your name?" Coach Jackson yelled as he pointed his clipboard at Keisha's big black bully ass.

"Who, me?" Keisha replied as she crunched on a bag of Flamin' Hot Cheetos.

She looked around, pretending as if she didn't know Coach Jackson was talking directly to her.

"Yes, you! Who else in the hell do you think I'm pointin' to? The air?" Coach Jackson huffed and rolled his eyes.

"Keisha Jermeka Jenkins! THE BADDEST BITCH IN THE CHI!" Keisha smacked as she clapped her chubby hands at every word spewing from her Flamin' Hot red-dye-stained greasy lips.

Her circle of besties chortled as they gave her daps.

"Okay then, Ms. Keisha Jermeka Jenkins, put the goddamn bag of Cheetos down and go give me three laps around the gym. NOW!"

"Man, I got asthma. I ain't gotta run." Keisha cut her eyes and continued to munch on the Cheetos.

"Girl, if you don't get yo' exercise-needin' ass up off that damn seat and give me my laps, I'm sendin' yo' ass to detention! And you know Ms. Thompkins ain't gon' let yo' asthmatic ass eat in there!"

Keisha smacked her teeth and quickly finished her Cheetos. Then she crumpled up the bag and threw it at the back of Summer's head. Keisha was sitting two rows above Summer.

"I'ma get you Skinny Red!" The bully got up and jiggled her way down to the court.

She started to jog, but after about a good ten seconds of jogging, her big ass gave up hope and walked the rest of the laps. Today was the start of the new quarter at Marcus Garvey and Summer was in her PE and health education class. As Coach Jackson continued to call attendance in the gym packed with

around fifty students, Summer heard one name that made her heart skip a beat.

"Zayn Hakeem."

She didn't realize her low-key bestie from English was in the PE class with her.

"Here . . ." Zayn lowly muttered as he raised his hand.

Summer looked over at him and smiled. He smiled back. After Coach Jackson got done calling attendance, he made the entire class run laps and then sent everyone back to the stands. Coach Jackson, like Mrs. Washington, was another carefree, burned-out teacher who just wanted to come to work, collect a paycheck and go back home to his couch, TV, beer, wife, and two sons. Unlike Mrs. Washington, Coach Jackson wasn't on the verge of retirement. He still had a good ten years left in the system. And honestly, he didn't give a shit about being a good teacher anymore. He already had his tenure and knew it would be hard for the district to fire his ass. After all the kids got settled back into their seats, everyone huddled up back up in their groups and cliques. Zayn sauntered over to a lonely, quiet Summer. She was reading a borrowed library copy of Maya Angelou's I Know Why the Caged Bird Sings.

"Hey, Summer" Zayn said.

He sat down next to her. She closed her book.

"Wassup, Zayn. I didn't think you were gonna be in this class."

"Yeah. Unfortunately. This is my second time in here."

Summer raised her brow. "Damn, you flunked PE? How you do that?"

"Long story. My moms got really sick so I kept missing school left and right to take care of her."

"Is she alright?" Summer asked, wondering if the rumors were really true, his mother really had full-blown AIDS.

"Nah, she's in hospice right now. She's dying from AIDS."

For a moment, Summer went silent and her mind blank. "I'm so sorry to hear that. I lost my mother too."

"Damn, word? I'm sorry to hear that too. How long she had it?" Zayn assumed Summer's mother died from AIDS.

Summer lowered her head. "Nah, she didn't die from AIDS . . . My father killed her and then killed himself. It was one big-ass accident. Over some random dumb shit."

Zayn got a bit tense, feeling a bit sorry he dug up a wound that hadn't completely healed. "Oh shit, my bad. I just assumed—"

"Nah, it's cool. Don't be sorry. It's life, right?"

"Yeah, I guess. Life of us niggas . . ."

This was truly the first time Summer and Zayn had the opportunity to talk face to face on such a deep level, getting to

really know each other. In English, the two mainly communicated through exchanging notes since Mrs. Washington rarely allowed her students to talk in class. Up to this point, the two didn't have any other classes together, and Summer couldn't interact with anyone outside of school due to Granddaddy's strict schedule of activities.

"Anyways, I don't wanna weird you out or anything, but over Christmas, I was thinking of you and got you a gift." Zayn suddenly pulled out a small wrapped gift and handed it to Summer.

"Oh my God, Zayn. You didn't have to do that." Summer was in shock.

She couldn't believe Zayn actually thought that much about her and went out and bought her a gift. Although she didn't really find Zayn necessarily full-on physically attractive since he seemed a bit geeky to her, just the idea alone of him buying her something when no one else did for Christmas was melting her teenage heart. She opened the gift. It was a fresh copy of The Rose That Grew from Concrete, an anthology of 2Pac's poetry. Elation wasn't even the appropriate word to describe just how Summer was feeling. The book just recently came out after 2Pac's death, and copies were selling for at least thirty dollars a pop—something Summer definitely couldn't afford. Granddaddy Luther didn't give her an

allowance of any sort. The only money he gave the girls was lunch money, and that wasn't even enough to buy her lunch every day, so she started bringing packed spam sandwiches to school to eat. A tear formed in Summer's eye. She reached in and hugged Zayn.

"Thank you so much! Where did you even get the money to buy this? Ahh, Zayn, you didn't have to do this!"

"Don't worry about it. Although I know we barely know each other, there's something about you I like . . . I mean, I'm not tryin' to flirt with you or anything, but you're cool as hell to me and we have a lot in common, so I figured I'd buy you it. Besides, it's just me . . . and my moms for now. I had some extra cash around the crib." Zayn smiled and hugged her back.

The two continued to chop it for the next hour or so until Coach Jackson dismissed the class. Summer didn't know what exactly would make of her growing friendship with Zayn, but she felt a growing attachment to him. He was giving her the peace of mind she longed for since moving back into the city. Summer was in the girl's locker room, changing out of her PE uniform and back into her regular school clothes. From a distance, she could hear Keisha and her group of besties running off at the mouth near the bathroom stalls and mirrors.

"Girrllll! You seen Rodney's big dick swingin' in his shorts when he was runnin' around the courts?" Sharday, one of Keisha's

friends asked her group of besties as she stood in the girls' locker room mirror, smoking a blunt.

"Yassss, bitch! I'll suck the meat off his shit!" Quiana, or as everyone called her, "QuiQui," barked.

"Girl, if you think he got a big dick, wait until you see Antwan's. Why you think they call him Jimmy Dean? That nigga's shit thicker than a sausage roll. You think you can stuff that down yo' throat?" Sharday chuckled as she passed the blunt to Keisha.

Keisha took two pulls and then blew smoke out of her wide nigga nostrils.

"Bitch, you know I loves to eat!" She laughed as she grabbed her stomach fat and jiggled it.

"Girl, hold this . . ." Keisha mumbled as she passed the blunt to QuiQui.

"MS. SKINNY RED BITCH!"

Summer slightly jumped when she heard Keisha shout her name.

Keisha sashayed her big ass toward Summer with one hand on her hip. Once she got super-close to Summer, she leaned on a locker, folded her arms, and looked Summer up and down.

"I'm hungry, Skinny Red. Let me get five dollars so I can buy me some snacks and shit from the vendin' machine."

Although Keisha was in the eighth grade, she was supposed to be in the tenth. She was the oldest student in the entire school, and most of the girls feared her. She and her besties were known as the "Lady Goons." You already know if some young ghetto bitches from the projects call themselves that, they are up to no good. Summer tried her best to ignore Keisha as she anxiously rumbled through her locker.

"I ain't got it, Keisha."

"YES YOU DO! I seen you get in yo' granddaddy's car! You stay with Reverend Gaines! He got money. All that money in the church! And y'all stay in Building 7! That's where all the boujee niggas stay. Now lemme hold five. I swear I'll pay you back! C'mon, girl!"

"Look, I told you I ain't got it, so stop fuckin' with me." Summer slammed her locker shut and walked off.

"Oh no, this skinny red bitch didn't! BITCH! I ain't done talkin' to you!" Suddenly Keisha lunged toward Summer, grabbed her by her long, curly hair, and slammed her against one of the lockers.

She held her hands against the lockers. The rest of the Lady Goons dashed over and helped Keisha pin Summer to the lockers. Sharday, who was still smokin' a blunt, blew a thick cloud of Smoke into Summer's face.

80

"BITCH! YOU FINNE GET HIGH TODAY!" QuiQui shouted.

While Sharday and QuiQui held Summer up against the locker, Keisha quickly went through Summer's pockets in search for cash. Other girls who were in the locker room passively watched, not wanting to intervene. They probably feared retribution from the Lady Goons.

"SKINNY RED BITCH! Three fuckin' dollars! That's all you got?" Keisha growled as she waved the dollar bills in her face.

Summer frowned and didn't reply. She was breathing hard and fast. If it was just Keisha here by herself, Summer thought she could've defended herself and took the risk to beat this fat bitch's ass. But because Keisha was flanked with her girls, Summer didn't want to take that risk and get jumped.

"I guess this will do. I really needed four so I can get me two extra honey buns. But I'll let you slide this time. NEXT TIME THOUGH! When I'm hungry, have my muhfuckin five dollars READY!" Sharday and QuiQui let Summer go.

The Lady Goons walked off laughing, back to the stalls to finish smoking their blunt.

"Weak-ass bitch!" Sharday echoed as the girls were back in their original spot.

A now angry, woozy-feeling, and slightly inebriated Summer

grabbed her belongings and stormed out of the locker to her next class. A few tears fell from her face as she sauntered upstairs to her last class of the day.

9

"Two hundred plus a thousand is . . . twelve hundred." Serena counted her fingers as she did her homework.

"Where da hell yo' grandmammy at? Tell her to come and brang her old ugly wrinkled ass out here and cook my GOD damn supper! Got me hungry as hell! Da hell wrong with her?" Granddaddy Luther growled to Summer and Serena.

As usual, he was sitting on his brown recliner in the living room, smoking a Newport, sippin' on some yak while he watched a rerun of Good Times.

"And why in the hell my house smell like polecat? Summer, are you getting' rid of yo' feminine napkins right, lil girl? Got my goddamn house smellin' like fishy coochie."

"Yessir, Granddaddy Luther . . . I don't know why it smells like that, but I'll make sure I'm getting rid of them properly next time, sir," Summer responded.

Maybe you smellin' that crack hoe pussy you've been bringing up in the house late at night, Summer thought, cutting her

eyes. It was Tuesday night. After the girls got done with choir rehearsal, they were sitting quietly at the dining room table doing their homework. Grandma Mary Hattie Mae usually would've had dinner ready by now, especially on Tuesday nights, because Grandma was supposed to make another one of Granddaddy's favorites: smothered giblets. It was a mix of chicken livers, hearts, gizzards, and kidneys sautéed with onions and peppers. Good ole country nigga eatin'. Serena got up and went to the back to go get Mary Hattie Mae. Summer continued to do her homework.

"AHHHHHHHHHHHHHHHHHHHHHHH!" Serena's screams blasted down the hallway.

Summer jumped and suddenly got up wondering why Serena was uncontrollably screaming. She raced down the dimly lit hallway and found Serena in their bathroom, still screaming, hovering over Grandma Mary's motionless body slumped over the small toilet. Summer grabbed her bawling sister and held her, trying to calm her down.

"Granddaddy Luther! It's something wrong with Grandma! COME!" Summer shouted as tears streamed from the corners of her eyes as well.

A minute later, Granddaddy came slowly strolling into the bathroom, a fresh Newport dangling in his lips, swirling his cognac in his glass, looking unbothered that his wife of over forty

years was unconscious and not breathing. The menacing patriarch took of sip of his yak, pushed the girls out of the way, and then leaned down into Mary's body. He ran his fingers against her neck.

"Summer . . . Go call an ambulance and tell 'em ya grandmammy's dead." Granddaddy stood up and then blew smoke out of his nostrils.

He took a swig of his beverage and then a long drag from the cigarette as ash sprinkled down his shirt.

"Goddamn. Old bitch dun messed up ma damn night. And when you get off the phone with them peoples, call up the pizza parlor and order me up a pizza pie. I want pepperonah, sausage. And uh, olives. And get me a large Pepsi cola. Hurry up too before they close." Summer and Serena, crying, still stood in disbelief Granddaddy Luther was so unmoved and unfazed by seeing his wife's lifeless, stiff body slumped over the bathroom toilet.

This nigga was crazy, and Summer now understood she wasn't dealing with just a stern, oppressive, so-called God-fearing disciplinarian. She was dealing with a psychopathic dope peddling hustler who was swiftly and surely revealing himself to be a fraud using God and church as a cover for whatever fucked-up bullshit he had going on. Venomous rage was now running a million miles an hour in Summer's blood. She wiped her face clear of her salty

tears and stormed down the hallway to the living room's house phone so she could call 9-1-1. Now although Summer never had a bond with her grandma, she still felt a lil sumpin' sumpin'. Shit, they barely exchanged words, but Summer still had the basic empathy to mourn the sudden, unexpected passing of a woman who was her family. Especially family who lived under the same Newport and chitlin smelling roof. Summer had been living with her grandparents for some time now and in actuality she began to feel sorry for her grandmother. Summer pitied Mary Hattie Mae. She probably had no other choice but to stay under Granddaddy Luther's dark and oppressive grip for decades, no questions asked. Death was probably Mary's ticket to freedom. Sweeter than this bitter life she had with Granddaddy Luther. Grandma Mary Hattie Mae died from a massive heart attack.

A day later, Summer was keen to how Granddaddy was moving so damn quick to throw Grandma in her grave. She found it odd, but then again, nothing was surprising her anymore. Granddaddy was one shady-ass, disgusting nigga. He slapped together some bootleg, simple funeral arrangements. You'd think if a man was married to a woman for over forty years, he'd want her to have a nice homegoing celebration. Nope. Not Granddaddy Luther Gaines. He didn't want anyone to order no flowers or bring any by the house. Shit, he didn't even want any visitors to come

by and give their condolences. One night when Summer asked Granddaddy about the janky arrangements, Granddaddy Luther told her, "Black niggas are too emotional. Let the dead bury the dead. Life is for living." And he meant every word because later that night he pounded Loretta's pussy to death.

And apparently Loretta didn't take enough fish oil that day, because her walls were cuttin' up Granddaddy's dick. Mary Hattie Mae died on a Tuesday and Granddaddy Luther was adamant on having her funeral as soon as possible—that Thursday! Most black folks had their funerals on Saturday, but Granddaddy told Summer there was no point in waiting just to throw someone's rotting body into the ground. It was fucked up big time. He didn't even give some of her distant cousins and other relatives enough time to make up it from Mississippi to mourn their kinfolk.

Besides, he told Summer, "I never cared for her trifling ass people. They ain't nothin' but harlots, thieves, and liars. Always callin' me for money. Da hell I look like? A charity?"

1:15 p.m. Thursday afternoon

Mexican cemetery workers rolled Grandma's cheap $300 pink casket down into the grave. Although the casket looked like it was made from Legos, he had the decency to get the casket in Grandma's favorite color. About fifteen people were in attendance, including Summer, Granddaddy, and Serena. The rest

of the folks were church members.

"C'mon, let's go. I'm hungry. Sister Bessie got the repast goin' at the church. She make good 'tayta salad too. You know, now that I think about it, I didn't like ya grandma's 'tayta salad. She used to make it too chunky. And then she always used to add too much relish." Granddaddy Luther ranted as he led the girls back to the car so they could get to the church for the repast.

Granddaddy was obviously hungry. As soon as the family got into the car, Granddaddy chucked the engine up and idled for a moment.

"Well, girls . . . That's life. The Lord giveth. And the Lord taketh away." He tapped his fingers on the steering while he dialed through different radio stations until he found the classic soul station.

The Stylistics' "Betcha by Golly Wow" blared through the speakers.

Granddaddy exhaled, "Anyways, I got company comin' in tonight from St. Louis. A good friend of the family. Since ya grandmammy's dead now, my lady friend gon help around the house to help me get situated. When we get back home, I want my house cleaned real good."

"Yessir, Granddaddy Luther," both girls muttered.

"Granddaddy Luther, can I ask you a question?" Serena kindly

asked.

"Yes, darlin'?"

"What's your lady friend's name?" Serena continued.

"Her name is Phyllis."

"How do you know her?" Granddaddy adjusted his rearview mirror, and looked back at Serena with his eyes turning to slits.

"Girl, hush. You know you ask too many questions . . ."

11:34 p.m.

The entire family rolled up to the Greyhound station in downtown. Serena and Summer were in the back, silent and a tad anxious, as James Brown's "This Is a Man's World" blared from the muffled car speakers. As Granddaddy drove closer and closer to the station, Summer saw about a good eighty people standing outside next to their luggage, looking around, waiting for their friends or family members to come pick them up from the somewhat sketchy-looking, dark passenger waiting area. Off in the cut, Summer gawked at homeless crazies roaming around like it was a zombie apocalypse. As Granddaddy Luther continued to slowly drive down the street with a square slapped in his mouth, he had his eyes glued to the crowd looking for his "lady friend," Ms. Phyllis. Granddaddy punched his big foot on the brake and threw the car in park.

He smiled and growled. "Phyllis."

"Be right back."

Granddaddy got out of the car and walked over to a woman standing off by her lonesome with two big blue suitcases next to her. The two hugged each other hard for about a good minute, and once Granddaddy released the woman, he leaned down and gave the woman a quick kiss on her lips and cheeks. Summer and Serena looked at each other in shock and slight disgust. It hadn't even been twenty-four hours since Grandma was sleeping in her grave, and here Granddaddy was kissing all up on some random hussy.

Summer rolled her eyes and hissed. "Ughh," she spat as she shook her head.

"Who is that, Summer?" Serena asked.

"It looks like some hoe-ass bitch . . . OOPS! Sorry, Sis. Just kind of livid right now," Summer apologized.

"Summer . . . I'm nine years old now. It's okay." Summer looked at Serena, smiled, and hugged her sister.

"I know, you gettin' all grown now, Sis." From a far, Summer tried to make out what this Phyllis bitch looked like.

She was brown, a bit on the slender side, wore a complete jean jacket outfit with a maroon T-shirt under it. She had this outrageous blond lace-front wig sitting on top of her head. Big fake gold earrings dangled from her ears matching the all of the

cheap jewelry she had around her neck and wrists. The two of them starting walking, Granddaddy behind her carrying her suitcases. As Phyllis got closer, Summer wanted to bust out laughing when she noticed Phyllis was cockeyed. This bitch looked crazy stupid to Summer. Granddaddy popped the trunk open and threw the suitcases in the back of the trunk. Then he walked over to the front passenger door and opened up the door like he was taking this bitch out on a first date. Da fuck! Summer thought, knowing she'd never, not once, seen Granddaddy open the door for Grandma. Shit, everywhere the family went Granddaddy made Mary Hattie Mae drive. Now this nigga suddenly was acting like Morgan Freeman in Driving Miss Daisy. Except the name of this movie was gonna be Driving Miss Phyllis. Once Phyllis plopped herself into the front seat, she turned around, looked at Summer and Serena, and smiled.

"DIS YO' GRANDCHURREN, LUTHA?!? Y'ALL ARE SO CUTE!" Summer was trying so hard not to bust out laughing in Phyllis's face.

Her eyes were scrambling all over the place like marbles, and Summer found it hard to look directly into the woman's aimless eyes.

"Yup, yup, dem is my grandbabies. The eldest is Summer. The other is Serena. These my daughter's churren. Y'all say hi."

"Hi . . ." both girls said lowly.

Phyllis reached her arm in and pinched Summer and Serena's cheeks. Instantly Summer wanted to throw up when she caught a whiff of rank fishiness on her fingers. Granddaddy chucked up the car engine and sped off, taking all four of them back to the Towers. Who was this bitch and why all of sudden did Granddaddy have this cockeyed hoe come staying with them, Summer wondered as she fiddled with her fingers.

10

"Bow ya heads," Granddaddy murmured.

As usual, he lowered his head and clutched his hands together over the table. Everyone else followed suit, even Phyllis. Fake-ass holy hoe, Summer thought.

"Lord, bless this food we are about to receive and let it be nourishment for our bodies. And we also ask that you bless the new addition in our home. In Jesus's holy name we pray . . . Amen."

"HALLELUJAH EIH SHALALA KO BA," Phyllis shouted, catching everyone off guard as she busted out speaking in tongues.

"Amen." Everyone whispered.

It was Friday evening. Luckily for the girls, they weren't subjected to some backwoods country bullshit Granddaddy made them eat normally. Tonight, the family was eating Popeye's. Summer figured since Phyllis was "new" company and had a little bit more pizzazz than her now deceased grandma, Granddaddy Luther was going to treat her and possibly Summer and her sister differently now. We'll see . . . Granddaddy decided to treat the entire family to Popeye's. This nigga splurged too. He dropped a

good fifty dollars on a twenty-piece spicy box, two large containers of Cajun rice, red beans and rice, green beans, and coleslaw. And then he bought a dozen butter biscuits, eight apple pies, and even stopped by Walgreens to get Blue Bell vanilla ice cream to go along with the apple pies. But that wasn't the only thing Summer noticed Granddaddy bought while on his Popeye's run. This nigga came back with a big bottle of Courvoisier and strawberry moscato. As the entire family ate and got down, it was almost as if the entire mood of the house shifted. Granddaddy Luther was showing a completely different, more gregarious side Summer found mindboggling. Granddaddy Luther was cracking jokes, telling crazy stories about his childhood growing up in Mississippi and his younger "sinnin'" days when he first moved to Chicago. He even let Summer have some moscato. Whatever was causing this shift, to an extent, Summer found it relieving. Maybe having Phyllis around wasn't a bad thing after all.

"Y'all wanna do somethin' this weekend?" Granddaddy asked as he stuffed a biscuit in his mouth.

Summer and Serena looked at each other, completely fucking puzzled.

"Like what?" Summer asked with a raised brow.

"I don't know. I figured I need to let up on y'all. Maybe I'll take y'all to the water park up north. BUT . . . That's only if y'all

SUMMER'S DIRTY LITTLE SECRET

stay on good behavior for the rest of the week." Serena jumped out of her seat in excitement and went and hugged Granddaddy Luther.

"Thank you so much, Granddaddy Luther." She then leaned in and kissed him on his cheek.

Now wait a minute? A trip? What the fuck was this bullshit? Summer thought, reluctant to wanna thank the man who just a couple of months ago chained her to a water heater pole and damn near starved her to death. She looked at her sister and then at Granddaddy.

"Thanks, Granddaddy Luther . . ." She fake smiled.

"You're welcome, sugar pie. Now, y'all clean up this mess, shower up, and get to bed. Me and Phyllis got some talkin' to do. Get nah before I change my mind." Serena, who didn't want Granddaddy to renege on the surprise trip, quickly stood up and started cleaning off the table.

Poor, naïve Serena, Summer thought. She didn't like the idea of seeing her baby sister get swindled into some bullshit. Her intuition kept telling her Granddaddy, and maybe even this Phyllis bitch, was up to no good. There had to be a reason why he was suddenly being so nice. After Summer and Serena got done cleaning off the table, cleaning the kitchen, and showering, the two of them shuffled to bed and drifted off to sleep. As Summer

faded away, she kept her mind alert of the fuckery looming in the near future.

Creak-Ca-Creak-Ca-Creak-Ca-Creak-Ca-Creak-Ca-Creak.

At 3:12 a.m., Summer woke up to the distant sound of Granddaddy's bed squeaking across the hall. She slowly made herself get out of the bed, curious as to what the sound was, but she slowly came into full consciousness. She already knew it had to be Granddaddy sliding in and out of Phyllis's pussy.

"AHHHHHHHH! Shit!" Granddaddy exhaled as he released a nut up into Phyllis's pussy.

Summer shook her head and made her way back to bed. Then suddenly she heard Granddaddy's bedroom door open and the two of them make their way down the hallway to the living room. Summer, looking to find out if they were about to spill the beans about their ulterior motives, waited for a good five minutes and then snuck out of her room. Once down the hallway, she hid behind the corner, ducked down, and had her ears glued to Granddaddy and Phyllis's conversation.

"So what you can do is, like I was sayin' before is, we can get that younger one on SSI for ADHD. They'll give her a script and er'thang. They'll put her in special ed., but you'll get a good check for $1,200 a month for her disability."

Summer's mouth flung open. She couldn't believe what she

was hearing. This bitch was consulting Granddaddy Luther on how to get Serena to fake a mental disability to collect a check from the government.

"$1200 a month . . . What 'bout Summer?" Granddaddy asked as Summer could hear him take a sip of a drink.

"It might be a bit hard with her 'cuz she a bit older and by now they would've diagnosed her. You already getting, what, $3,000 a month for takin' care of them? Hell, I'd put her ass on the block."

"Nah, not yet. She might be able to do runs for me though . . . Hrrm, but now you got me thinkin' . . . I had to light that lil nigga up the other night. Young dumb nigga. I think he go to Summer's school too."

"Damn, Luther . . . You killed a kid?"

"Hell yeah. I don't give a shit. Nigga tried to steal from me. You know I don't play that, baby. But Summer . . . I'm gonna have to think about that one a lil bit 'cuz she a lil smart lil sneaky-ass girl. Just like her damn mama. She might try to play me. And if she play me, I'm gon send her ass off just like I did her mammy."

"Where you put the body? Ain't the boy's parents lookin' for him?"

"Bleh, that nigga ain't have no mama or daddy. Well, a mama . . . That bitch on dope though. Got AIDS too."

Phyllis chuckled.

Summer's heart began to race. What "kid" was Granddaddy Luther talking about? From the description of it, it sounded like it could've been Zayn. Zayn did tell Summer his mother was a drug addict, a heavy heroin user who got AIDS from using dirty needles. And then Zayn bought Summer that 2Pac. Is that how he got his money? Was he working for Granddaddy and didn't even realize Luther was her grandpops? Summer held her mouth, almost wanting to cry and shout because she hoped it wasn't Zayn who Granddaddy Luther possibly murdered. Since her grandmother died, she had not been to school for the last couple of days and had no way of getting in touch with Zayn. She got up, tip-toed back to her room, jumped in the bed, and cried herself to sleep, hoping that her friend wasn't the one Granddaddy killed.

11

Thunder and lightning clapped outside as Granddaddy Luther finished preaching. After Granddaddy collected his fifth love offering for the day, church let out.

"You sho' preached a good sermon, Reverend Gaines!" Brother Horton, one of the church's longtime members chatted up with Granddaddy Luther.

On this rainy afternoon, for some odd reason, church attendance was thicker than usual. There were about a good forty members here today. Through the entire service Summer was so torn up on the inside. Since Friday night when she eavesdropped on Granddaddy Luther and Phyllis's conversation, her mind stayed worried about her friend, Zayn. And to make her fears even more fucked up, she knew Granddaddy had a larger agenda at play and this Phyllis bitch was here all along to help him carry it out. But this time, Summer wasn't going to be idle anymore. She was gonna figure this shit out and use every bone and muscle in her body to fight her way through this. She'd be damned if

Granddaddy was going to try to use and exploit her and her sister for whatever it was he had going on. And now that she knew these two niggas were on some trifling bullshit, she needed to know just how deep Granddaddy was in the dope game. Was he working for someone? Or was he running shit himself? She had questions and she was going to get her fucking answers. After about a good twenty minutes after the service ended, Summer and her sister got up from the small choir stand and made their way to the front door of the church. After exchanging a few words with a few older members, Summer noticed a young, tall nigga walk in with a head full of dreads and hundreds of tatts etched all up and down his light brown neck and sleeves. He was wearing jeans, a pair of purple Jordans, and a long white T-shirt. Obviously this nigga wasn't here to get his soul saved. To Summer, he looked like the typical dope boy she'd often see hustling in the Towers.

"Reverend Gaines . . ." the young nigga said, immediately catching everyone's attention.

The church folk suddenly paused conversations they were having among each other and turned their heads toward the unfamiliar voice as they gawked at the young, off-putting guy. Most of the church members were around Granddaddy's age, give or take, so the flat, somewhat nervous looks on their old brown and black faces weren't surprising. They probably wondered in

fear who this young "thug" was and why he called out "Reverend" like that. Was he about to do something bad?

"Jashawn!" Granddaddy smiled and shouted back to the young guy. "It's alright, everyone. I know this young man."

Granddaddy then patted Brother Horton on his ninety-five-year-old frail hump back, "Be right back, Brotha Horton. Lemme see what this young man need."

Granddaddy coolly walked over to Jashawn standing next to the front door and then gave him handshake. As Summer and Serena made their way to Phyllis, who was chatting away with Sister Bessie, Summer kept her investigative eyes glued to Granddaddy and the young thuggish lookin' Jashawn as the two of them appeared to be enthralled in deep, quiet, intense exchange. A minute passed, the dude exited through the front door, and Granddaddy sauntered his way to Summer.

"Sorry to interrupt, Sister Bessie, but we gotta go on 'head and get. I gotta take care of some thangs at the pantry."

"Oh, no worry, Rev. I was just tellin' Summer and Phyliss how I found this new brand of chitlins out of Walmart that come precleaned. Save Ms. Summer here lotta time cleanin' them chitlins now that Mary Hattie Mae dun went on to glory." Sister Bessie laughed and pinched Summer's cheek.

"Thank ya, Sister Bessie," Granddaddy said then looked at

Phyllis.

"Go on and take Serena back to the apartment. I'm gonna take Ms. Summer with me to go to the pantry. They havin' some issues down there."

"I can help, Reverend. These chilluns look hungry. Y'all hungry?" Sister Bessie asked as she looked ready to help Granddaddy Luther down at the food pantry.

"Yesss . . ." Serena and Summer responded.

But Summer knew this was some straight-up bullshit. Ain't no goddamn "issues" going on at the pantry. With anxiety laced in her bones, she was amped to see if Granddaddy was gonna really take her to the food pantry to fix whatever it was going on.

"No worries, Sister Bessie. We gotta move some serious boxes and they weigh kind of heavy. I'on want you to hurt yo' back," Granddaddy replied as he gripped Summer's shoulder.

"And Miss Summer here is a strong lil gal. Phyllis and Serena, I'ma have Brotha Horton take y'all back."

After leaving the church, Granddaddy and Summer hopped in his Cadillac and made their way to the Pilgrim's Way Food Pantry on 79th Street. This was the same food pantry Granddaddy Luther made Summer and Serena volunteer at during the holidays. It was managed by Father Flake, a white Catholic priest who was around Granddaddy's age.

"Summer, go and do me a favor, baby doll," Granddaddy muttered once they pulled up and parked on the side street next to the pantry.

"Go and give that box of Nilla wafers in the back to Father Flake. He's gonna give you a thick manila envelope too." Granddaddy pointed to the back seat.

Summer looked back at a huge box resting on the leather back seat. On their way to church earlier this morning, Summer noticed the case wasn't in the back seat, and now all of a sudden it was there. Summer's eyes widened. Something was telling her there wasn't no damn wafer cookies in that box.

"Okay, Granddaddy Luther," Summer replied as she got out of the car.

Once she opened the back car door, she grabbed the box and carried it to the front door of the pantry. Luckily it had stopped raining about a good hour ago, so she didn't get wet as she stood at the door with the slightly heavy box in her hand. She hoisted the box onto her hip and held it with one arm, quickly knocking on the pantry's big red door three times with her free hand. Granddaddy was still in the car, smoking a cigarette as usual, eyes glued onto Summer. Seconds later, Georgette, one of the pantry's workers, opened the door and led Summer in.

"How you doin', Summer? I ain't seent you in a while! Girl,

you gettin' so grown!" Georgette beamed as she led Summer down to Father Flake's office.

"I'm doin' fine, Ms. Georgette."

"How's school?"

"It's good. Can't complain."

"Good. So good. I love to see young black churren succeed in school. Don't be goin' off, messin' around with these dirty-dick boys. They ain't nothin' but the devil!" Georgette laughed.

"Haha, I won't, ma'am . . ." Summer chuckled.

Finally making their way all the way back through the stale-smelling, dusty, dimly lit food pantry, the two women arrived at Father Flake's office, his door already opened. He was sitting down, reading, classical music blaring from a small black radio on his desk.

"Father Flake. Summer's here for you," Georgette announced.

Father Flake closed his book and put it down on his desk.

"Summer! Nice to see you again! Where's Reverend Gaines?" He got up from his desk, walked over to Summer, and took the box out of her hands.

"He's still inside the car . . . smoking a cigarette."

"Ohhh. Oh okay." He raised his brow looking a bit confused. "Well, give this to him. Tell him I said have a wonderful Sunday afternoon!" He handed Summer a thick manila envelope.

Just what Granddaddy Luther told her to get in exchange.

"I will. You have a wonderful day as well, Father." He smiled, didn't say anything back, and just went back to his seat, sat down, picked up his book, and started reading again.

Summer walked out of his office with Georgette right next to her side.

"Tell yo' granddaddy I'm comin' to visit his church for Easter Sunday."

"I will, ma'am," Summer responded as she gave Georgette a light hug and walked out of the front door of the pantry.

Once she made her way back into the front passenger seat of Granddaddy Luther's Cadillac, she handed Granddaddy the envelope. He rolled down his window, took a long pull from the Newport and threw the finished cig out his window. As Granddaddy Luther opened the wrinkled, used-looking manila envelope, Summer had her unblinking brown eyes fully zoomed in to his black, ashy hands. What was Granddaddy about to suddenly pull out? If it was a cash, especially a bunch of it, Summer knew she'd have her first piece of evidence to know for sure this corrupt, old black nigga was up to no good. And boom! There it was—Granddaddy whipped out a stack of crispy cash wrapped in a thick red rubber band. After sliding the band off the stack of cash, Granddaddy quickly ran his fingers through the

money, lowly mumbling, staring off into nowhere in particular as he kept a mental count.

"That lyin', cracka-ass mothafucka! I knew it!" Granddaddy growled once he counted the last one-hundred-dollar bill.

Summer's nerve-racked body shuddered at the sound of Granddaddy slapping his heavy right hand against the Caddy's steering wheel.

Granddaddy grabbed Summer by her yellow dress collar and looked deep into her eyes, "Listen here, Summer! If you ever tell anyone what you 'bout to see, I'll kill you, you understand me, lil girl? I'll kill you and Serena."

"Yes, Granddaddy Luther," Summer fearfully responded.

"Now get out, don't say a fuckin' thing, and just watch . . ." Granddaddy screeched. Summer's heart raced.

Granddaddy Luther leaned forward, opened the glove compartment, and snatched out a silver flask and a silver long-barrel .38 revolver. Summer's chest tightened at the sight of Granddaddy sitting the heavy-looking gun on his lap. What in the fuck is about to go down? Summer wondered as her breathing intensified. Granddaddy opened the flask, took a swig, and growled.

He handed Summer the flask, "Drink the rest of it! You gon' need it."

Summer took the flask out of Granddaddy's hand and quickly attempted her best to effortlessly down the bitter brown cognac. Her head spun and pounded as the dark liquor ran down her throat and burned her esophagus. She wanted to immediately throw up the second the alcohol entered her tiny, empty, hungry stomach. But she knew she might solicit an unwanted, possibly violent reaction from Granddaddy if she displayed any signs of weakness or revulsion if she didn't throw that shit back like a pro. The second she got done, she put the flask back in the glove compartment and closed it. Granddaddy quickly checked the cylinder of the gun, making sure he had all seven rounds ready to go. He spun the cylinder and slapped it back in place.

"Get out!" he roared as he swiftly got out of the Caddy and slammed the door.

Summer followed suit. Once out of the car, Granddaddy grabbed Summer to his side.

"Stay by my side." He put his hands behind his back, hiding the gun from plain view.

The two of them walked up to the pantry.

"Knock . . ." Granddaddy commanded Summer.

Summer knocked three hard times on the rickety red door. Seconds later, Georgette slowly opened the door and popped her head through the slit.

"Reverend Gaines! So nice to see ya! What y'all still doin' here?" Georgette fully opened the door with a big smile on her face.

"Hey, Sister Georgette! Ohhhhh, nothin' . . . I just need to have a word right quick with Father Flake. How's Lonnie doin', by the way? He still workin' down at the Sears? Now that boy is too old to be workin' on them cars!" Summer could tell Granddaddy was making fake conversation to distract Georgette.

"Yeah, I tried to get him to retire, but he said workin' keeps him young! Come on in. Father Flake's still in the back." Georgette laughed as she creaked the door open and let Summer and Granddaddy in.

As the two trailed behind Georgette, Granddaddy quickly looked around. "Who else workin' today?" he asked.

"Oh, it's just me and the Father here," she replied as she strolled down, leading them to Father Flake's office.

"Good . . ." PLOP! Granddaddy pulled the gun from around his back and slammed the handle of the gun into the back of Georgette's head.

Summer jumped and her mouth flung open the second Granddaddy's pistol whipped the gregarious woman. She wanted to cry, but again, she knew had to keep her composure. The plump, older woman fell face flat onto the floor. Granddaddy leaned down

and pistol whipped her again twice, but this time harder, making sure he rendered her completely unconscious, if not outright dead. He stood up, looked down at the motionless pantry worker, and let out a chuckle as he put his hands on his hips.

"Now let's find that lyin', lil-boy-dick-lovin'-ass cracka . . ."

12

Knock! Knock!

"Come on in . . ." Father Flake muttered behind his office door.

Granddaddy Luther opened the door and coolly strolled in with his revolver visible for the father to see.

"You know . . . I always knew you were a shady-ass mothafucka . . ." Granddaddy growled with Summer at his side.

Summer looked at Father Flake, whose face was now painted with pale terror. She was so stunned an unassuming man like Father Flake would be involved in Granddaddy Luther's secret drug operation. The father dropped his Shakespeare book on his desk crowded with folders and paperwork and slowly raised his quivering, clammy hands.

"Reverend Gaines . . . What's this about?" he screeched with his gawk concentrated on the gun aimed at his torso.

"You know what the fuck this is about . . . This is the third time you've been short on the count. And I had someone watching yo' peckerwood lil-boy-dick-fondlin' ass for weeks now," Granddaddy Luther bellowed as he inched closer into Father Flake's presence, pointing the gun directly into his chest.

"Are you a snitch?" Granddaddy raised his sweaty brow.

Father Flake nervously laughed. "No, no. I'm not a snitch! But Reverend . . . About the money. I can explain. I really can. See, I needed to wire my brother some money in Vegas. He owes the mafia a lot of money."

"I. Don't. Give. A. Fucckk. About yo' brother. I don't care if ya mammy needed money for heart surgery. I run a business. You work for me. You should know never to steal from your boss." Granddaddy suddenly smiled and put his gun down to the side.

"You must think I'm some old dumb black nigga, white boy."

"No, I don't think that," Father Flake cried. "Oh . . . Please don't kill me, Reverend! I promise I won't fuck up again."

"You know my policy on three strikes. And why are you scared? You know what the fuck you signed up for. Besides, it ain't like you got a wife or kids. You don't even like pussy. What kind of man don't like no pussy? You know, Father Flake, back when I was growin' up in Mississippi, I used to know this boy named Reggie. Reggie Green." Granddaddy pulled out a chair in front of Father Flake's desk and sat down and kicked his feet up on the desk.

He continued to rant as he fiddled with his revolver. "There was somethin' really odd about Reggie. He wasn't like the rest of us boys. Didn't like goin' outside. Always stayed up under his

mammy's titty. Loved to cook. Loved to sew. Always played with dolls. Me and my friends used to tease him for actin' like a lil-ass sissy. When we all got older, Reggie kind of shook that shit off and started doin' more manly stuff. Played football. Worked in the fields. He even had him a lil ole girlfriend."

Summer just stood there, flabbergasted Granddaddy Luther suddenly got so goddamn cozy and comfortable, telling his crazy-ass childhood story. Her small heart continued beating a million beats per minute and she just wanted this dark afternoon to be over. She now knew she had to escape quickly and get her and her sister out of this man's secret and dark underworld. Seeing this entire situation unfold before her eyes solidified her knowing Granddaddy was a straight up psychopathic drug peddling killer and there was no way in the hell she was going to endure Granddaddy's psychotic madness any longer. Her mind raced, thinking of so many ways she could leave.

"Years later, after I had left Mississippi, I remember I came back one year to bury Mama. I went into Jackson to go cash Mama's life insurance policy, and guess who I ran into . . . ? Reggie. Except he wadn't Reggie Green no more. He was Father Green. That boy dun became a priest. We talked for a minute, and later that evenin' 'Father' Green invited me over to his house for supper."

After we got done eatin', we drank some bourbon and talked about our days growin' up in Hattiesburg. One thing led to another, and you know what Father Green did?"

Father Flake, still quivering, looked fearfully at Granddaddy. "What?"

"He reached in and touched my dick. And guess what. I didn't flinch not an inch. I whipped my big black dick out and let him suck up and down, all night long, until I came all down his throat."

WHAT! WHAT. THE. FUCK! Summer's eyes widened as Granddaddy confessed to letting another man suck his dick.

Father Flake gulped. "What happened next?" he asked.

Granddaddy closed his eyes and snickered. "He wanted me to fuck him in the ass . . ."

"Did you do it?"

"No . . ." Granddaddy pulled out his pack of Newports, whipped out a cig, slapped it in his mouth, and lit up. He took two drags and blew smoke into Father Flake's face. "I killed him."

Father Flake gulped again.

"Lemme explain sump'in to you, Father. I ain't a fag. And I don't like 'em either. Especially the fags hidin' in holy clothin'. I can't trust no fag 'cuz y'all think like womens. Run yo' mouth. Gossip. Complain. Lie. Steal. My daddy always told me, too, you catholic priests were some crazies. My daddy told me no man in

his right mind would give up pussy for Jesus. And now I see why Daddy said that. Cuz I'm lookin' at a lyin'-ass, no-good fag right now."

"No, Reverend. Please. I'm not gay."

"SHUT UP!" Granddaddy barked. "You gon prove it to me." Granddaddy looked over at a frightened Summer. "Summer, sit down . . . We gon be here for a while." After Granddaddy Luther got done telling that insane story, he called up his secret crew to the pantry.

Three guys—Jashawn, Black Rob, and Lil Curt—showed up, ready to get down to business: torture the shit out of Father Flake to get answers out of him. Granddaddy also told them to bring Loretta to the pantry. Why in the fuck did she need to come, Summer wondered. For the last few months Granddaddy suspected Father Flake had been an informant for either the police or the feds. Father Flake denied the allegations, but Granddaddy believed him to be lying. He had Jashawn spying on Father Flake, and on numerous occasions the young worker saw Father Flake going into an unmarked car with a middle aged-looking white male who Jashawn claimed looked like a straight up jake. Out of Grandaddy's crew, Jashawn was the youngest. Black Rob and Lil Curtis looked like some old-school gangsta niggas from the late '70s. Black Rob, well, Summer knew why he got that name,

because he was tall, black, and had a wet Jheri curl. Lil Curtis was short, skinny, and had a perm and a gold front. Summer figured they had to be in their fifties. She was slowly piecing together everyone involved so far with Granddaddy's operation. First starting with Loretta. Summer quickly determined more than likely Loretta was an elite veteran crack hoe, neighborhood lookout, and beta tester for new dope. Loretta was cluck bitch who had her ears to the streets listening in for the latest street nigga news. Then there was Father Flake. Summer now knew the pantry was being used as a front to push dope into the streets. And it made perfect sense since so many crackheads and dopeheads often came to food pantries looking for "assistance" in a time of "need." Father Flake was probably on Granddaddy's payroll for a minute. Using a white Roman Catholic priest was the smartest shit ever since they don't usually fit the profile for a drug dealer and no one would ever suspect a pantry would also be used as a trap house. Phyllis—well, Summer hadn't figured out her MO yet, but based on prying into her conversations with Granddaddy Luther, she figured Phyllis was probably running an operation down in St. Louis. She was probably also a scamming bitch who knew the ins and outs of how to do bank fraud, crack credit cards, and also defraud the welfare system. That would explain why she recommended using Serena as bait to get money out of SSI. With

Summer now being introduced to Granddaddy's "crew," she already knew what the deal was with these niggas. But there was one other question that lingered in the back of her mind. Did Grandma know all along what Granddaddy was up to? Did she play a role? And then, what about other members in the church? Were they in on this entire scheme? Granddaddy made Summer watch every single second in this crazy fucked-up movie called Summer's Life. A movie Summer, truth be told, didn't want to see.

"Father Flake . . . meet Loretta. Loretta. Meet Father Flake," Granddaddy introduced the two characters.

Under any normal circumstance, two individuals who'd never met before in their life would shake hands. But not this Sunday afternoon. Granddaddy's crew stripped Father Flake down, tied his pale, saggy, hairy ass to an old wood chair, and had duct tape wrapped around his eyes.

"Heyyy, Fatha Flake!" Loretta rasped through her sunken-in mouth with her bony hands in her dirty jeans pockets.

She was dressed in one of her usuals—a dirty off-white "Miller Family Reunion" shirt, a pair of jeans and torn up white sneaks. She still had that one braid in her hair. Father Flake didn't happily greet Loretta though. He was uncontrollably crying, shivering in his seat, wondering what tragedy was about to befall

him next.

"Please, Reverend. I swear. I can fix this. Please."

Granddaddy Luther walked closer to the father in his seat, leaned down, and whispered in his ear, "When's the last time you got yo' dick sucked, white boy?"

"Wh-hha-aat?" Father cried.

"Loretta, come suck this white boy's dick . . ." Granddaddy commanded.

"Ewww, Luther! You got me fucked up! He ain't even got no damn dick. That shit look like a lil-ass crawdad. Babay! I only suck on big ole hammers."

"Bitch, I didn't give you an option. Get this cracka dick hard. I wanna know if he likes gettin' his wiener sucked on . . .'Cuz I think he's a fag!" Loretta rolled her eyes and got down on her knees, right in between Father's legs.

She tickled his shrimp dick for a second and then dived right in, attempting to get Father's small white hairy dick hard. Everyone studiously watched, including Summer, who was feeling super-woozy from watching everything go down. She honestly didn't know what to think anymore. A minute or two passed.

"This cracka ain't getting hard, Luther!" Loretta spat. "Fuck this shit! A bitch gotta be somewhere!"

Granddaddy, who was standing feet away with his hands on his hips and a Newport in his mouth, chuckled. He had gotten the confirmation he needed.

"I knew it. You ain't nothin' but a sodomizin' homosexual," Granddaddy muttered as he gave Jashawn, Black Rob, and Lil Curtis a nod.

The crew quickly untied Father from the seat, and then with all of their explosive strength and power, threw him onto a table in the middle of a foldable pantry in the middle of the table. As the father lay there on the table, face down, the guys grabbed the father's arms, placed them behind his back, and slapped handcuffs on his wrists. Granddaddy Luther calmly walked over to a corner in the bright room, snatched up a brown broomstick from the corner, and coolly strolled back to the table. He took two more drags from the cigarette, threw it on the ground, and put it out.

He leaned down and began whispering. "Father . . . You got one more opportunity to tell me if you've been talkin' to the police."

"Boss! I swear, I haven't been snitching! I swear!"

Granddaddy quickly ripped the duct tape off of Father's eyes and scarily looked at him, smiling, "Oh yeah, so who were you gettin' in that unmarked car with every day at around 9:30 p.m.?"

Father Flake couldn't even look Granddaddy Luther in his

eyes as he wept. After a few seconds of no response, he wailed, "His name is Gary. He's a male escort."

Granddaddy chuckled and shook his head as he waved the broomstick in front of Father Flake's widened teary eyes. "So you do like dick up yo' ass . . . Just like I thought."

"C'mon, Reverend! Please!" Granddaddy walked to the opposite side of the table where Jashawn and Lil Curtis steadily held the Father's bare pale legs down. The scared priest tried to fight against their grip.

"Spread them legs, faggot-ass cracka!" Granddaddy Luther hawked some spit in his hand to lubricate the broomstick.

Seeing as how this was about to get really fucking nasty and she couldn't take it anymore, Summer ran up to Granddaddy Luther and grabbed his arm holding the stick, "Granddaddy Luther! Please. This is too much, bro!"

Granddaddy Luther grabbed Summer. "WHAT DID I TELL YOU EARLIER IN THE CAR? NOW GO BACK OVER THERE AND WATCH!" Granddaddy growled as he threw her back to her spot.

Summer tried her best to resist tears seeing how Granddaddy was about to do something horrible and disgusting to Father Flake. Without hesitation, Granddaddy rammed the pool stick up Father Flake's ass.

"AHHHHHHHHHHHHHHHHHHH!!!"

Granddaddy continued to pillage Father Flake's ass until he went unconscious.

Granddaddy threw the bloody broomstick down on the ground and whipped out his revolver. POW! POW! POW! POW! POW! POW! POW! Summer shuddered at the thunderous pop each time Granddaddy Luther shot at Father Flake's naked body, emptying out the entire chamber of bullets.

"Somebody clean this shit up before we open up for breakfast tomorrow. These white college students comin' down here tomorrow to volunteer." Granddaddy stuffed the gun back in his waist. He looked at Summer. "Let's go, baby girl. You hungry?"

With her eyes slightly teary, she shook her head in an indiscernible direction. "Ye-ea-ahhh."

13

"Welcome to Popeye's! Can I take your order?" the Popeye's drive-thru cashier blared through the bright red menu's speakers.

Granddaddy didn't go to the Popeye's right around the corner from the Towers. He decided to take a trip up to the North Side. He preferred at times to take the extra drive because he felt like too many trifling niggas worked at the one around the corner from his apartment.

"Yeah, lemme get a two piece, spicy, Cajun rice, extra biscuit with an extra side of coleslaw." Granddaddy looked at Summer. "What you eatin', baby doll?"

"Can I have the number five, Granddaddy Luther? With an extra biscuit as well?"

"Yeah, lemme also get a number five with an extra biscuit."

After getting the food and making their way back to the Towers, Summer couldn't take it anymore. She started crying as she looked out the passenger seat window.

"Why you over there crying?" Granddaddy asked, sounding as usual unsympathetic he'd just subjected his granddaughter to raw, unfiltered violence. "Cut all that hollerin' out."

"Can you please just tell me what's going on? Tell me the truth, Granddaddy Luther. PLEASE! WHY! Who are you!" Summer begged as crocodile tears flooded her face.

Granddaddy suddenly pulled over on the side of the street and threw the car in park. He cracked his knuckles and rubbed his goatee. He then reached into his shirt pocket, whipped out a cig from his almost-empty pack of Newports, lit it up, and took a pull. Once he blew smoke out of his nose, he looked over at Summer.

"Nate . . . Big Nate. Yo' daddy. He used to work for me. And he betrayed me. Not only did he steal my money . . . But he stole my daughter. Your mama."

"What?" Summer sat in shock at the new revelation.

A new revelation that now had her all twisted up. Her father used to work for Granddaddy Luther?

"But I thought you were a pastor. Granddaddy, you sell drugs."

He chuckled. "That's a front. All one big-ass, good front." He took a pull from the cigarette.

He looked at Summer and pulled the pack out from his shirt. He pulled the last cigarette out from the pack and handed it to Summer. "You want one?"

Summer slowly shook her head no. "It's bad for you."

"Who gives a fuck? We're all gonna die one day." He

laughed. "Here, I got somethin' better." Granddaddy opened the front console, pulled out a small mahogany wood box, and opened it up.

Summer looked down at the box. This old black corrupt nigga had eight pre-rolled joints tightly packed against each other. He took a joint out, sparked it up, took three puffs, and passed it to Summer.

"Is that weed, Granddaddy Luther?"

He choked and punched his chest. "This some good-ass shit. Take a hit. It'll get yo' mind off what you just saw."

"Granddaddy Luther . . . No, I can't do that."

"Girl, if you don't smoke this goddamn weed!" Granddaddy suddenly flipped mad and shoved the joint into Summer's face.

She took the slowly burning joint out of his big hand and took a light puff. Other than getting that contact high from when Sharday, one of the Lady Goons, blew smoke in her face, this was the first time Summer smoked weed. The smoke didn't even fully make it down her throat and into her lungs, and she started to cough really bad. Granddaddy laughed, and oddly enough, rubbed her back to help her get the plume of smoke out of her virgin lungs. Summer began to feel heavy, high, and dizzy. Slight paranoia began to invade her slender body and she could feel her heart pound as if an African warrior was beating on it like a drum. All

her senses were heightened to a thousand. She didn't know if she should enjoy the feeling or be frightened of it.

"This is some good loud right chea . . ." Granddaddy Luther took three more puffs from the joint and then passed it back to Summer.

She took more puffs, this time getting better and better at holding the smoke in her lungs. The deep feeling of being high totally hijacked her body. Sadly enough, her paranoia subsided and she found the feeling from the weed to be calming and relaxing. Granddaddy didn't go straight back home. He pulled off into a random parking lot in South Loop so the two of them could eat. Summer always knew that when people smoked green they'd get the munchies. She always thought it was a joke, but now that she had THC running in her bloodstream, she was hungrier than a motherfucker. Oddly enough, as the two ate, they listened to the radio and Granddaddy cracked jokes about how he hated the new music out.

"I can't stand that Poof or Puff Daddy or whatever the fuck name he got. What young niggas call him? And why he mumbles all the time? And he got a big-ass mouth with that weird overbite. Boy got all that money and won't even get his mouth fixed."

Summer laughed. Not because what Granddaddy was saying about Puff Daddy's mouth was true, but she found it ironic that

he'd make such a shrewd comment about Puffy's mouth given Granddaddy's teeth were all brown from years and years of smoking cigarettes, drinking black coffee, and sipping on brown yak all day long. After the two got done eating, they got rid of the trash and headed back to the Towers.

"Phyllis's stank coochie ass probably wonderin' where the hell we at."

"Granddaddy Luther, can I ask you another question?" Summer calmly asked, still enjoying her high.

"Yes, baby girl?"

"Why did you suddenly show up? I am just so confused. We never met you before. Mama barely mentioned you. I am just so confused about everything."

"You want the short answer or the long answer?"

"I prefer the long answer. I'm not Serena."

Granddaddy chuckled. "Well, the long answer is this. I used to be the biggest kingpin in Chicago. I ran everything from 18th down to 130th Street. I used to have everything on lock . . . even the towers. Your father used to be one of my good, young lieutenants. I trusted him. I taught him everything about the game. I loved him like a son. But he was planning on trying to take me out to take over everything, and he swindled your mama into believing it."

"Daddy tried to take over?"

"Yes, so my people chased him out of the Towers. But once he got on his own, he got smart. Really smart, and eventually he took out all my people and took over everything . . . Left me penniless."

"Can I ask you another question?"

"This is your last one . . . I'm tired."

"Why did you wanna take us so bad? Serena and I were so happy up North. I am just so confused. Why bother with us?"

"Because . . . since your father stole from me, I'm stealing from him. Y'all belong to me now. And I'm gon make y'all work until I get back every single dime that lyin'-ass-nigga father of yours ever stole from me. I'm on a mission to get back on the top. Now, Summer, I'm gon leave you with this for the night. You can either help me or hurt me. But you can't really hurt me, so you ain't got no other option but to help me. Once I get what I need to get back to the top, you can leave . . ."

"What? You want us to work for you? Sell drugs?" Summer's high quickly evaporated at Grandfather's last utterance.

All of these deep, secret, family revelations coming to light shredded her to pieces. She felt so conflicted because now she had a different picture of her father, and even of her mother, painted in her mind. She knew her father was a dope king, but she never

knew the circumstances surrounding how he even got involved. Nate kept her shielded, not wanting to delve too deep into his history in the streets.

"Yes, sell my damn dope. You do right be my, I'll take care of you. Fuck me over, I'll kill you. We got an agreement?" Granddaddy's voice returned to his normal dark undertone.

"Granddaddy Luther—one last question . . . Please, I promise this will be it."

"Summer . . . after this, that's it. If you got more questions, save 'em for the morning."

"Did Grandma ever know about all of this?"

Granddaddy chuckled. "Yeah, that dumb bitch knew. And for your information, lil girl, that wasn't your grandmammy. That was your great aunt. Your grandma's sister. Your real grandmother, Dorothea, my real wife, she died giving birth to your mother. Your mama never knew that. You're the first to know."

14

*"**Shamaya Gates . . .**" **Coach Jackson lowly muttered as he*** checked off his attendance roster.

"Here . . ." the light skinned girl with Poetic Justice jumbo braids chirped.

"Zayn Hakeem . . ." Silence.

"Zayn Hakeem." Silence once more.

"Porscha Higgins."

"Here . . ."

It was 1:35 p.m. Summer bit her unpolished nails as she desperately scanned the gymnasium's crowded stands looking for any traces of her friend Zayn. He wasn't in English class this morning and now that Summer was in PE, Summer noticed he was still nowhere to be found. She fought against shedding tears because she didn't want to believe the possibility Zayn was the kid who Granddaddy Luther murdered. She wanted to ask Granddaddy Luther last night if he too killed Zayn but she couldn't muster up enough strength to do so. She'd already seen and heard enough, and still needed time to process everything. Her feet rapidly tapped against the gym stands as she held out hope

any second now Zayn would come strolling through the doors looking unfazed with his usual black hoodie on, glasses slapped against his face. This past weekend was truly a scene out of a Chicago slum ghetto version of The Twilight Zone. Truth be told, to Summer, this was an experience far worse than witnessing her mom and father's bloody senseless deaths. Now that Granddaddy Luther confirmed he was nothing more than a corrupt, murderous drug dealer using the church as a way to push dope and reclaim his glory in the streets of the Chi, Summer realized she had to quickly prepare herself mentally and emotionally, probably even physically, for a rollercoaster of events most likely about to occur in her young tumultuous teenage life. Summer, along with Serena, needed to work for Granddaddy to pay back a longstanding debt her father, Big Nate, incurred while working for the OG kingpin Granddaddy Luther. She didn't know exactly what this work would entail (although she knew it was going to involve drugs), but now her top concern was what role Serena would play in all of this. She was more than willing to make the sacrifice if it meant her and her sister's way out, but she did not want her baby sister to be exposed to all of this raw, unfettered murder, violence, and dope peddling. Another revelation that threw her back was finding out Mary Hattie Mae wasn't her real grandmother. Summer was really upset by this revealed piece of information given her

deceased mother didn't even know the truth about her real mother. She also wondered just who exactly Mary Hattie Mae was and why she spent so much time under Granddaddy's grip without saying a word. And then of course, another worry still floating in the back of Summer's mind was the entrance of this scammin'-ass Phyllis bitch into her life. She was going to have to deal with her eventually.

After Coach Jackson got done calling attendance, he made everyone in the gym run laps. Once the students got done, Summer returned to her seat in the stands and opened up the 2Pac book Zayn gave her not too long ago. Her eyes watered once she flipped to the page containing those first words Zayn exchanged with her:

The power of a gun can kill, and the power of fire can burn. The power of wind can chill, and the power of mind can learn. The power of anger can raise inside until it tears you apart. But the power of a smile, especially yours, can heal a frozen heart—2Pac.

A few of her salty tears dropped into the page.

Summer smiled, closed the book, and then closed her eyes. She could see Zayn's smile, warming her heart. Deep down inside, her heart desperately hoped her friend was okay, and she just needed to be patient and keep smiling.

"SKINNY RED BITCH!" Keisha shouted as she stood in the middle between her Lady Goon squad, clearly asserting herself to

be the leader of the pack of ghetto wolves.

Summer was back in the locker room getting ready to leave and go to her last class. The last time she encountered these bully bitches, she told herself to quickly get ready and head out, but it seemed like today Keisha and the girls had fucking with Skinny Red Bitch Summer on the top of their agenda. Summer panicked, quickly grabbed her stuff, and tried to make a dash for the exit of the locker room. But she wasn't quick enough. Sharday lunged toward Summer, grabbed her by her hair, and dragged her back toward the lockers.

"LET ME GO! LET ME THE FUCK GO! Someone please go tell Coach Jackson Keisha'nem fucking with me!" Summer shouted and begged, hoping a few of her remaining classmates would intervene and go get help from Coach Jackson.

But those fearful little girls lowered their heads, remained silent, and pretended like they didn't hear Summer.

"LET ME GO!" Summer continued to scream, hoping perhaps her screams would echo out of the girl's gym locker room and then to Coach Jackson—shit, at this point, anybody.

"SHUT THE FUCK UP, BITCH! YOU DOIN' TOO MUCH!" Keisha bellowed as she pushed Summer up against the lockers.

Sharday and QuiQui pinned Summer to the lockers, holding

131

her hands out.

"THE REST OF YOU BITCHES NEED TO GET OUT NOW!" Suddenly, at Keisha's command, all the girls remaining in the locker room got up and quickly made their way out.

Keisha chuckled as she pulled out a blunt from the back of her ear and sparked it up. She took a huge puff and held it in her mouth. She leaned in, grabbed Summer's face, and then locked her plump, purple, blunt-stained lips onto Summer's. She blew smoke into Summer's mouth as she continued to passionately kiss her. Of course Summer resisted. She fought to keep her mouth tightly, closed but Keisha's mouth overpowered hers. Sharday and QuiQui laughed at the sight of Summer resisting Keisha's smoke kiss.

"Skinny Red Bitch, you know you like it!" QuiQui mocked.

The second Keisha released her lips, Summer erupted into coughing as plumes of smoke fell out of her mouth.

"I'm hungry Skinny Red . . ." Keisha spat.

"Take her pants off and spread her long-ass legs. Lemme see what this bitch taste like." the lead, vicious, unbothered bully commanded as she coolly stood there watching her sidekicks go at pulling down Summer's pants and panties.

Summer now was ready to fight. She'd be damned if she was gonna let these bitches try to fondle or rape her. She ferociously

further into Summer.

"Oh, oh . . . You still a virgin? I thought you was jumpin' on Zayn's dick. He look like he got a little dick anyways . . . I think my brother might like this though . . ." Keisha pulled her fingers out of Summer, smelled them, and then sucked on them like they were strawberry Blow Pops.

"Damn, you taste good. Spread them bitches, Goons. When I get done, y'all can get a taste too!" Keisha then got on her knees and dived her head into Summer's crotch, fondling the virgin, nubile girl's private parts.

After Keisha got done munching on Summer, both Sharday and QuiQui took their turns getting a five-minute taste of Summer's young, pink, untapped slit.

"If you ever tell anyone about this, bitch . . . I'll fuckin' kill you! You understand me, Skinny Red Bitch? I fuckin' kill you," Keisha laughed as she took the boxcutter out once again and gently dug the tip of the knife into Summer's cheek, giving her a small laceration. "Let that be a muhfuckin' reminder."

15

"Phyllis, I'm takin' Summer wit me to go handle some business. Look after Serena and make sure she do her studyin'." Granddaddy Luther stood by the door as he slipped on his black leather jacket.

Granddaddy had some important "business" to take care of, and Summer needed to be there. Now that Mary Hattie Mae was dead and there was no one in the house to teach the girls how to sew and crochet, Granddaddy was gonna use this Thursday afternoon to teach his eldest granddaughter and new employee something else. Summer was anxious, right at the door, ready to go. Granddaddy Luther took his favorite black red feather fedora off the hat rack, put it on top of his black bald shiny head, and then cocked it to the left like a pimp.

"And when you gon learn how to cook a meal, woman? I'm tired of eatin' Popeye's. You been in my house for over a week and you still ain't cooked me a hot meal yet."

It wasn't even 5:00 p.m. yet and this trifling Phyllis bitch was

wearing a red night robe and a big-ass black satin bonnet. She sauntered from the kitchen with a burning Virginia Slim in one hand and a cup of moscato in the other. She took a puff from the cigarette, cut her googly cock eyes, and took a sip of her chilled alcoholic beverage.

"You know goddamn well I don't eat that nasty shit you had that slow country bitch cookin'. You got me all the way fucked up if you think I'm gonna clean chitlins. You better get Summer's lil red ass over there to do it. I'm not the one!"

Granddaddy Luther's faced screwed up. He grumbled as he shook his head. He walked over to Phyllis, who was now standing next to Serena near the dining room table. Granddaddy whipped out his wallet and slammed a fifty-dollar bill on the table.

"This the last night we eat Popeye's! Tomorrow, make sure yo' ass cook up my pork chops. And next time you get flip with me like that, I knock them eyes straight. You understand me, bitch?"

Phyllis took a puff of her cig, blew out a stream of smoke, and then slowly sashayed over to Granddaddy. She leaned in, kissed him on the cheek, and slapped his ass. "Sorry, Daddy," she chuckled with a tinge of seduction laced in her words as she walked off to the den.

Serena, sitting at the dining room table doing her homework,

giggled as she observed the entire awkward interaction between Granddaddy Luther and Phyllis. Granddaddy wasn't feeling Phyllis's seductive vibes. He rolled his eyes and huffed.

"Stank hoe," he whispered under his breath, and then turned his attention to Summer.

"You ready, baby doll?" he asked Summer, smiling.

"Yup . . ."

P-I, M-P, ology, but logically

We learnin' these hoes biology, and obviously, well

Do you want to ride?

In the backseat, of a Caddy

Chop it up with Do or Di—

Granddaddy changed the radio to his favorite soul station. James Brown's "Payback" lowly blared through the Caddy's speakers. He turned down the volume to a level likeable to his ears. Then he opened his leather jacket with his right hand and whipped out a pack of Newports as he commanded the steering wheel with his left. Once he got a cigarette slapped in between his long purple lips, he lit up the cig, took two long puffs, and stared off into the afternoon cityscape.

Summer was already drifted off, staring out of the passenger window to nowhere particular. She was still reeling from the trauma of being sexually assaulted by the Lady Goons. Between

Granddaddy Luther's madness, the constant bullying of the Lady Goons, and worrying about Zayn, Summer was beginning to contemplate suicide. She was to the point where she was so blank and delusional, she'd convinced herself she'd rather kill herself and go to heaven to be with her parents and maybe Zayn than to be living in this current hellish nightmare called reality.

"Summer, Summer, Summer . . . I got a surprise for you, baby girl." Granddaddy smiled and glanced at Summer.

She didn't say anything in response. She was still staring off through the window, arms folded, body kind of leaned to the side.

"What's wrong? Something wrong?"

Summer turned and looked at Granddaddy Luther. "It's nothing. Just thinkin' about school. That's all."

"That's good. Stay in school. I wish I would've. I dropped out in ninth grade to go work in the fields. Why you think my hand's so hard and heavy? I used to pick cotton from 7:00 a.m. to 8:00 p.m., Monday thru Saturday."

"Wow, that's long. I can't imagine," Summer replied.

"Yeah, you don't wanna imagine. That's why I moved to Chicago. So I can have a better life for myself, your grandma, and your mama." Summer noticed Granddaddy's face turn a bit soft, signaling to her Granddaddy was expressing a more emotional side to himself that up to this point she'd never seen.

Now was the opportunity for her to ask some other questions lingering in her mind. "Granddaddy Luther . . . Did you ever love my mother?"

He didn't say anything in response. He continued to smoke his square. He looked at Summer, and his eyes rapidly blinked as if he was trying to avoid shedding tears.

"Yes . . . Yes, I did love her. Of course. She was my only child. My only daughter. Why wouldn't I love her?"

"Then why did you kick her out if you loved her?"

"I didn't kick her out. She left with your no-good, lyin' daddy. Got in her mind."

Summer paused her line of questioning. She fiddled with her hands and stared at the dashboard, ready to ask another question but needing to word it correctly. "Granddaddy Luther . . ."

"What?"

"Please don't get mad when I tell you this. But the other night, when Ms. Phyllis came into town, I woke up and heard you all talkin' in the living room. She said she was gonna try to get Serena on psych meds to get money. Are you gonna allow her to do that? Please, Granddaddy. I'll do whatever it takes to not let her do that. Serena doesn't deserve that. None of this. Please, Granddaddy. Don't make her sell or do anything else."

Granddaddy chuckled as he kept driving. "I knew you were a

nosey-ass girl. What else you heard?"

Now was the moment to ask the question she'd been longing to ask. "The boy you killed. What was his name?"

Granddaddy's eyes turned to slits. "Why you wanna know?"

"I think I knew him . . . Was his name Zayn?"

"Oh, so you had you a lil boyfriend, I see." Granddaddy finished his cigarette, rolled down his window, threw out the butt, and rolled the window back up.

"I knew that little nigga. And yes . . . I killed him. Had to."

"Why! Why, Granddaddy? WHY!" Summer cried and screamed.

"He was my friend!"

"Summer . . ."

"You killed him! He was so nice to me! He was my only friend at school and you killed him!"

"SUMMER! THAT'S ENOUGH! NOW SHUT UP!" Granddaddy silenced Summer's shouting.

She buried her head in her hands and kept crying. Although she had final confirmation over Zayn's unfortunate fate, she still wrangled her mind over why it had to be Zayn. Why not someone else? Granddaddy pulled over on the side of the expressway.

He looked at Summer and slowly reached his hand toward her. "Summer . . . Baby doll. I'm sorry. I didn't know he was your

friend."

"But why, Granddaddy? Why?"

"He stole from me. A lot, actually, and there's one thing I don't like. Thieves. And I'm gonna give you some good wisdom here, if ya daddy ain't gave you any. If a nigga lies to you, he'll steal from you. And if he'll steal from you, he'll kill you. Zayn worked for me, and I took good care of him and his mama, and he lied and stole from me. Ain't no tellin' what he'd do next . . ."

Summer kept shaking her head in disbelief. "This is so unreal."

"It's business, baby girl. It's just business. And I had to take care of business." Granddaddy put the car back in drive and took off on the expressway.

"Where are we going?" Summer asked once she saw the sign on the expressway letting her know they crossed the Illinois-Indiana state line.

"Gary, Indiana. I got a surprise for you there. I think you'll like it." Granddaddy laughed.

16

Granddaddy Luther pulled into a parking lot of what appeared to Summer to be a massive unused warehouse on the east side of Gary, Indiana. She assumed the warehouse wasn't in use given the amount of uncut shrubbery and tall green grass that surrounded the massive building. Once Granddaddy cut the car ignition off, the two got out and began walking, Summer following Granddaddy's lead. Summer looked around and noticed two other vehicles—a Lincoln Town Car and a white utility van—parked far off near the docking area of the warehouse. Obviously, there were other people here. She wondered who was inside, but she knew whoever was also here had to be working with Granddaddy.

"This is where the surprise is at?" Summer asked, turning her face up at the sight of the tall patches of brownish green grass that grew from the concrete in the parking lot.

"Yup. You gon' love it too. And I hope you prepared to take some good-ass notes 'cuz you gon need it when workin' for me," Granddaddy mumbled as he puffed on a cigarette.

Summer didn't respond though. Her eyes suddenly found themselves absorbed by a small pink and purple cosmos flower

with a tiny yellow bulb in its center sprouting from a crack in the parking lot's concrete. Enamored by the odd presence of the flower, Summer's mind quickly drifted to 2Pac's poem, "The Rose That Grew from Concrete," instantly reminding her of her short-lived friend, Zayn. Granddaddy continued to walk on, but Summer had to stop the second she saw the flower. She leaned down and delicately plucked he flower as she recited in her mind the words to the poem:

> *Did you hear about the rose that grew*
> *from a crack in the concrete?*
> *Proving nature's law is wrong it*
> *learned to walk without having feet.*
> *Funny it seems, but by keeping its dreams,*
> *it learned to breathe fresh air.*
> *Long live the rose that grew from concrete*
> *when no one else ever cared.*

"Summer, what in the hell are you doin'?" Granddaddy barked once he realized Summer wasn't behind him. He stopped and put his hands on his hips. "C'mon, it's gettin' late already, damn it."

"Sorry, Granddaddy Luther. I just saw this pretty flower," she

said as she held the flower up to her button nose, taking in its faint sweet fragrance.

A tear slowly crept from the corner of her eye. "I'll always love you, Zayn," she whispered to herself.

Although her and Zayn never had the chance to seriously get close in a romantic way, she was almost on the precipice of giving her young, innocent heart to him if he gave her an invitation to his love. She hurried back to Granddaddy's side. Once they arrived at a side entrance of the warehouse, Granddaddy knocked three times. Seconds later, the door creaked open.

"Boss man . . . Y'all finally made it," Lil Curtis said as he further opened the door, allowing Granddaddy and Summer in.

"Hey there, Ms. Summer. Pretty flower."

"Hey, Mr. Curtis," Summer responded and nervously smiled.

Once inside, Summer's assumptions were instantly proven wrong. The warehouse was definitely in use. The moment her and Granddaddy walked in, her eyes attached to the vast, bright warehouse space lined with rows of stacked shrink-wrapped cardboard boxes sitting on pallets. The smell of cardboard box, Pine-Sol, and fresh paint invaded her tiny nose. As she continued to scan the area, off to the far end of the warehouse floor, she saw a large group of at least twenty women, sitting down at what looked like four foldable tables put together. Most of the women

were brown or black, with one or two blond white girls in the mix. Summer then noticed the young women were topless and had on medical face masks, gloves, and hair nets. As Summer, Granddaddy, and Lil Curtis walked closer and closer toward the group of females, she speculated most of the women sitting down were between the ages of fifteen and twenty-five. Goddamn. How big of an operation was Granddaddy running, Summer wondered as they finally arrived at the group. Summer studiously watched the large group of women sitting silent, working fast, stuffing baggies with red and yellow vials out of large containers lined down the tables. All types and sizes of titties were exposed, their nipples hardened from the blast of cool air streaming from large room fans connected to a small rumbling generator.

"Girls . . . Stop for a moment. I want you to meet our newest employee, my oldest granddaughter, Summer." The topless female employees abruptly stopped what they were doing, pulled down their face masks, and waved at Summer.

"Hey, Ms. Summer," most of them said in unison.

"She's gonna be workin' with us?" one girl, who looked to be around Summer's age, asked.

Oh hell fuckin' no, Summer thought. She'd be damned if she was gonna spend her spare time stuffing baggies with dope and crack rocks. Although she knew she was gonna be involved in the

dope game one way or another, Summer didn't exactly think it would entail this.

"Nah, I got her workin' on another project. Something I think she'll be good at." Granddaddy smiled and patted Summer on her back.

"Anyways, y'all get back to work. We're under a deadline. Y'all finish up by midnight and I'll kick back an extra bonus."

"Yessir, Reverend Gaines . . ." the girls all responded together. They then pulled their face masks back up to their mouths and went straight back to work.

"Right this way, Summer," Granddaddy commanded. "You gon be in for a world of surprise." Granddaddy and Lil Curtis led the way, Summer following behind them.

She looked back at the girl who asked if she was going to be working right beside her. Summer wondered where the girl was from and what happened in her life that led her to working for Granddaddy in this isolated warehouse, off in the middle of the nowhere, stuffing baggies with death with her small brown titties out like it was nothing. Summer then turned her attention back to the two older men and followed them down a staircase leading to a basement. As she walked down the stairs, nothing but fear and nausea blanketed her body as she walked further and further into what seemed to be complete darkness. Once down in the

basement, Lil Curtis opened a door. Faint dark-red light beamed the area. An all-out anxious Summer followed her Granddaddy and Lil Curtis through the door and then turned the corner. They slowly strolled down a damp, moldy-smelling hallway illuminated by a single dark red light. By this point, the sound of the rumbling generator mixed in with the dozens of girls stuffing plastic baggies was replaced with the sound of water dripping from several water pipes running along the sides of the brick walls and ceilings.

"Granddaddy, where are we going? What's down here?" Summer inquired as they kept walking, maneuvering around puddles in the ground.

"Patience is a virtue, Summer." Granddaddy growled.

His voice now returned to the familiar dark, oppressive, vicious tone, reminding Summer of the first time he inflicted violence on her. Summer didn't respond. She just kept walking until they all arrived at another door. Lil Curtis opened the door, and once they walked inside, Summer instantly knew what time it was. She saw three niggas, completely naked, on their knees with light blue pillowcases over their heads. They were kneeling down on clear plastic tarps, their bodies shivering hard. They were trembling because not only was it cold like a fucking freezer down here, but it was obvious by their battered and bloodied bodies they knew they were moments away from getting knocked the fuck off.

Granddaddy walked up to the guy positioned in the middle with his hands behind his back.

"Summer, you're about to find out the real reason why your daddy killed your mama and then himself. And you're also about to learn somethin' you'll carry with you for the rest of your life."

Summer took a huge swallow as she deliberately unfocused her eyes, trying her best to not get a glance of the naked men and their exposed privates. She wanted to throw up all over the place, but again she had to quickly remind herself now wasn't the time to display fear or weakness. Any glimpse of that shit would mean she'd be on the ground, naked with a pillowcase over her head as well. Granddaddy snatched off the pillowcase and threw it to the side.

"UGHHH!" Summer gasped and suddenly held her mouth as her now widened eyes attached themselves to the family face.

Quan. Her once godfather and Big Nate's best friend. Also, number two in command within Big Nate's organization. Although Summer hadn't seen Quan in years, her eyes became teary as emotions flooded her slender, shivering body. Her chest tightened and her heart raced a million miles per hour the second she realized Quan's eyes had been completely gouged from their sockets with nothing but bloody, dark emptiness in their place.

"Summer, is that you, baby doll?" Quan cried as his head

turned left and right as if he could really see her.

"Nigga, shut the fuck up. Don't act like you miss her and shit. After all, you're the one who's responsible for her parents' deaths," Granddaddy Luther barked.

"Summer, come here . . . I want you to get the truth on why yo' daddy did what he did to my daughter, your mouther, and then pulled the trigger on himself . . . Go on ahead, Quan. Confess."

"Luther . . . please, she don't need to hear all of that. She's too young to understand," Quan begged and quivered.

Summer's world became upside down at hearing this new dark revelation. Her godfather had a role to play in sparking her father to commit a murder-suicide? Summer walked closer up to Quan and looked at Granddaddy Luther with tears and fear in her doe eyes.

"Granddaddy, Quan . . . What are you all talkin' about?"

All of sudden Granddaddy grabbed Quan by his short afro, "Tell 'em, nigga. It's the RIGHT thing you could do before you die."

Quan shrieked, "Please, Luther. Come on, bro. I swear. I'll just disappear and go away for good and just hand over everything to you."

Granddaddy chuckled. "I already got everything, dumb nigga. Now we can do this the easy way or the hard way. You're gonna

die regardless. The question is do you wanna die a long, slow death if you keep fuckin' around, or do you just wanna go out with one big bang? You make the choice."

"Man, Luther. I told you honestly it was one big mistake."

Granddaddy Luther looked at Lil Curtis. "Hand me that taser."

Lil Curtis walked over to a table that was laid out with all types of guns, knives, and other tools of torture. Once he grabbed the long baton stun gun off the table, Lil Curtis chuckled and handed Granddaddy Luther the stun gun. Granddaddy Luther playfully waved the stun gun around as he sparked it up, flashes of blue electric flames bouncing in the air, their cracking sounds echoing in the damp, muggy basement.

"Dis here a twelve-million-volt, military grade triple stun gun baton. Cost me $99.99. No sales tax applicable, nigga," Granddaddy growled as he leaned into Quan's ear and ran the baton up and down his taco meat chest-hair-riddled chest.

BUZZ! BUZZZZZZZZZZZZ BUZZZ! "AHHH! AHHHHHHHHHHHH!" Quan screeched, and his naked body violently shook as Granddaddy dug the round end of the stun gun into Quan's neck.

"This is fun. Summer, you wanna try?" Granddaddy smiled as he asked Summer and kept chucking up blue electric flames from the baton.

Summer slowly and nervously shook her head no as she kept her mouth covered in utter disbelief. BUZZ! BUZZZZZ-ZZZZZZZZ BUZZZ! BUZZ! BUZZZZZZZZZZZZZ BUZZZ! Without hesitation Granddaddy shoved the baton down into Quan's crotch, this time electrocuting him for a longer length of time. Quan shook and screamed as frothy, bubbly foam formed at the corners of his bloodied mouth.

"You ready to speak, you lyin' nigga?" Granddaddy asked Quan.

"Su-mm-mmmer . . ." Quan lowly cried. "I'm ss-sss-sooorrry, baby girl. It didn't ha-aa-ve to happen this way."

Summer looked at Granddaddy and then at Quan. Granddaddy Luther beckoned her over to get closer to Quan.

"She's standing right in front of you. Now tell her the full story before I drive this pole up yo' hairy, shitty ass," Granddaddy commanded.

"You remember when Big Nate went to prison, Summer?" Quan asked.

"Yes," Summer responded as tears flooded her light brown cheeks. "Yes, I do."

"Well, I tried to take over things . . . For good. Me, Boone, and Juice wanted to get rid of Big Nate."

Summer's teary doe eyes looked to Granddaddy. "What?

What do you mean?"

"Aisha was Big Nate's weakness. Y'all was his weakness. Always was. He loved y'all too much. Way too much that it stood in the way of us gettin' things done and making more money. Boone and Juice put it in his ear that I tried to mess with yo' mama. We knew it would drive him crazy. I thought he was gonna confront me about it. Then I was gonna kill him and claim self-defense. But instead, he first went straight to yo' mama. He got too high and went crazy. That's why he killed her."

Summer's eyes reddened and more tears rushed out of her eyes like waterfalls. "Goddaddy! All over a lie. ALL OVER A FUCKIN' LIE! 'CUZ YOU GOT GREEDY!" Summer screamed.

"Sorry, baby doll. It wasn't supposed to happen that way."

"RIGHT! It wasn't. And now my mama's dead. My daddy's dead. Me and Serena's lives were uprooted 'cuz you got greedy. 'Cuz you, Boone, and Juice wanted more money!"

Quan didn't respond. He just kept quivering in silence. Granddaddy leaned down into Summer's ear.

"You see what I said about liars. They will steal and then kill."

Summer's blood was boiling at a thousand degrees with rage and hate. Hearing this confession, which inevitably was the final piece in the puzzle in explaining why her father did what he did, was the flame igniting the bomb of vengeance buried within

Summer's slender, fourteen-year-old body. She was ready to explode and kill everything in sight.

"Here are the two other co-conspirators, Juice and Boone," Granddaddy growled, snatching off the pillowcases from off the two heads. Granddaddy leaned down into Summer's ear once more. "So what do you wanna do, baby girl? You wanna learn how to get revenge?"

All Summer saw was red. In her retribution-filled mind, the walls began to bleed crimson. The floors were painted in blood. She looked at Granddaddy with her face now tightened and her eyes turned to slits. Her breathing got fast. So fast Granddaddy looked at her chest and could see her small yet plump teenage titties attached to her chest go up and down. He chuckled—he knew Summer's lesson in revenge would become her initiation into his clandestine mob.

17

"I wanna kill them, Granddaddy Luther. I want them gone!"
Summer growled.

She was now heavily drunk off Granddaddy's killer spell, and all she wanted was to murder. The words "murder, murder, murder" in her eyes were written everywhere on the thick cement walls of the basement. Granddaddy Luther snickered as he folded his long arms.

"Y'all hear that? Summer's ready to kill you dumb black niggas." Granddaddy looked and nodded to Lil Curtis.

"Before we get started, we first gotta teach you how to shoot a gun. Big Nate ever taught you how to hold a gun, Summer?"

"No. No, he didn't. But I'm ready to learn," Summer replied robotically with her eyes attached to the three assailants responsible for the destruction of her family.

"I'm ready to fuck these niggas up."

"Good, good, good. That's what I wanna hear," Granddaddy responded.

Lil Curtis walked over to the table laid out with guns, knives, swords, and other crazy shit. He picked up a gold .50 Desert Eagle,

walked back over to Granddaddy, and handed it to him.

"I love the sound of a bullet crackin' a nigga's skull wide open," Granddaddy growled and smiled.

"Lil Curtis, go get the rest of the guys so we can hang these niggas up on the walls like Picasso paintings." At Granddaddy's command Lil Curtis dashed out of the room to get the rest of the crew.

Minutes later, Jashawn and Black Rob and some other unknown members of the crew came busting through the doors, read to tie these fuck niggas up. They took each guy, one by one, and dragged their tied-up bodies to the other end of the basement. Then, they stood all three guys up against the wall, their naked bodies fully spread apart to give young future killer Summer enough canvas to land a hit. With their hands already tied, the guys were hung from water pipes running on the ceiling of the basement like cow carcasses ready to be sliced up into prime cut steaks.

"Summer. First, I'm gonna teach you how to aim and shoot to kill." Granddaddy loaded the gun with an extended clip. He sniffed the long barrel of the gun and growled, "I love the smell of fresh steel. This shit I'm finne teach you you'll carry with you 'til the day you leave this muthafuckin' earth." Granddaddy Luther leaned down and opened up Summer's hands and slid a gold Desert Eagle into her soft hands. "You feel that? This ain't

nothin' but one hundred percent pure revenge, baby girl. I'ma teach you how to put a bullet in between each of these fuck nigga's eyes. Every time you see their heads blow back, you'll feel alive. You ready to feel alive?"

"Yeah," she mumbled as she slowly shook her head with her mouth hung open.

Truth be told, she began to feel a tad terrified. For the first time in her life, deep down inside, she knew this was going to be the day and very hour she was going to go from being a naïve, innocent, nerdy girl to a soulless killer. Her childish wide-open eyes looked up at Granddaddy Luther. He produced the biggest smile she'd ever seen. He looked down into her eyes, all of his rotten teeth open to examine. This was the first time he beamed such a huge smile to his eldest grandbaby. Jashawn ripped the pillowcases off Juice's and Boon's heads. They looked at her with such intense, disappointing stares. It was like they knew their end was coming and coming at the hands of a young, fourteen-year-old girl who was seeking to avenge her parents' deaths. Granddaddy Luther guided her hands up to Juice.

"Tuck your arm against the side. You're gonna feel that recoil. Now aim at this dumb nigga. Yup, yup, yeaaaaah. Riiiiight there. Right in between his eyes. Now blow him the fuck away."

Her small finger slowly squeezed the trigger. She was scared,

but ready. Ready to put these niggas to sleep. POW! Summer's body flew back as the gun blasted. The loud, reverberating sound knocked her hearing out of commission, and she could barely hear what her Granddaddy was uttering. But she looked at his lips and could tell he was saying, "Good job, baby girl. You ready for the next?"

She nodded her head in agreement. Seeing that fuck nigga's head fly back along with bits of his skull, speckles of pink brain, and burgundy bubbly blood splashing all over the ground like paint on fresh canvas was exhilarating to Summer. Giving a low-life fuck nigga instant death gave Summer instant life. Granddaddy was indeed right. The explosion of the gun was like a high no man could ever fathom. She now understood each shot she was about to take was going to be like a shot of fresh, raw, uncut dope being injected in her arm, shooting her up with the high of blissful vengeance. She moved onto her next target— Boone. But this time Granddaddy removed his hands.

"No need for training wheels anymore. You got this, Ms. Summer. I see it in your pretty eyes."

She aimed the gun at Boone's chest. She closed her left eye. Zoomed in. Right into his center left. She anticipated the powerful recoil. She gripped the gun harder and hoisted it carefully so she wouldn't fall back again. Boone looked at her. He tightened mouth

and held his head up high and closed his eyes. POW! With the blast of the gun, Summer's body barely trembled. She was getting very good at this art of vengeful murder. With the instantaneous gun shot, Boone's head suddenly dropped. A huge, smoky wound in Boone's chest oozed blood. Granddaddy Luther stood in awe that his grandbaby was perfecting her shot. She now was on her final target: Quan.

"Wait . . . I don't just wanna kill him quickly like that. That's too easy," Summer spat.

Granddaddy chuckled as his slowly rubbed his goatee. "So what you wanna do? Torture him?"

"Fuck yeah," Summer growled. "Fucking torture his treacherous ass."

Suddenly the newly fomented assassin Summer walked over to the table of weaponry. She searched and scanned the portfolio of weapons, knives, and other torture accessories. She picked up a sharp hunter's knife. She looked at the knife and flipped it side to side as light from the ceiling light glistened off its tip. She laughed and then sauntered right in front of Quan's naked body. She looked him up and down as she ran the tip of the sharp knife down from the middle of his chest to his navel. Once she arrived at his belly button, she growled, "I'm finne turn yo' ass into a bowl of chitlins."

"AHHH! AHHHHHH! AHHHHHHHHHHHHHHHHHH!" Quan screamed as Summer, without warning, viciously speared the sharp hunter's knife deep into Quan's abdomen.

She drove the knife deep into him, until she could almost feel the vertebrae of his spine touching the tip of the knife. She jiggled the knife a bit as blood gushed from the deep wound, splashing Summer all over her face and body. It didn't bother her though. She kept going. The more she saw blood the more she pumped the knife in and out of the man until there was a foot-long puddle on the floor. The second she got done jiggling the knife deep within Quan's insides, she pulled the knife out halfway and then began to cut and saw out a large, round portion of his abdomen. As she got close to slicing off a large circle from the middle of his abdomen, suddenly his bloody, slimy sack of intestines plopped to the floor, making a sound that made Summer laugh like a fucking lunatic. The sound brought her back to the time she first learned how to cut through the fat and membrane of chitlins. Jashawn and Lil Curtis looked at each other, and then quickly rushed to the girl, wanting to intervene, to keep her from sinking too far into the abyss of her vengeful madness.

"Hey! Let her keep going . . . She knows what she's doing . . ." Granddaddy chuckled as he stopped the two from restraining Summer.

Summer looked over at Granddaddy and smiled. She dove right back in, completely cutting out Quan. Once his intensities, liver, and stomach were on the ground, she leaned over and played with the bloody organs on the ground like they were Play-Doh. She squished a few of the intestines in her hands, got up, and looked at Quan, who was now seconds away from death.

"Open up, nigga. I'm gonna feed you your own shit. OPEN UP!" Summer crazily screamed. Quan slowly opened his shivering mouth.

Summer then force-fed the man his own intestines. She opened her hands and dropped the rest of the guts in her hands and wiped her hands on his body. She took the knife, pulled on his flaccid dick, and sawed it until it was completely detached from his body.

"Here's dessert," she muttered as she stuffed the man's flaccid dick in his mouth.

His head collapsed and Summer now knew he was dead. She went back over to the table and picked up the gun. She stood back a distance from of all of the bodies, zoomed in, and went at it.

"HAHAHAHAHHAHAH!" POW! POW! POW! POW! POW! POW! POW! POW! POW! POW! POW! POW! POW! POW! POW! POW! POW! POW! POW! She laughed and screamed as she emptied the clips onto all of the guys' bodies.

She kept pulling the trigger despite there being no more bullets. Granddaddy knew it was time to conclude today's lesson, strode over to Summer, and took the gun out of her hand. Unexpectedly, her crazy, demented laughing transformed into sobs and cries as she wrapped her bloody hands around Granddaddy Luther and hugged the man with absolute love, devotion, and obeisance as if she had loved him for an eternity.

"Thank you, Granddaddy. That was the best gift anyone could've given me."

"I know, baby girl. I know . . . You did good. I'm proud of you." Granddaddy hugged her and chuckled.

Summer had officially crossed over the burning sands, now finding herself to be a certified hitta or an assassin in Granddaddy's operation. The once innocent, naïve to the world mind of Summer's was gone the moment she landed a bullet between Juice's big forehead. The shadow of revenge all of sudden made her long forget about the initial abuse and torture she suffered at the hands of the violent, oppressive Granddaddy Luther. She was now beholden to the corrupt and morally bankrupt man as her savior and redeemer. He offered her salvation and redemption through the gun, and now that Granddaddy gifted her the sweetest revenge, she pledged herself to commit any act of murder at his command. All along Granddaddy knew what he was

doing. He was, after all, the one who planted the plot in Quan's mind. Granddaddy spent the next two hours teaching Summer everything she needed to know about guns. Using the lifeless bodies as targets, Summer went on to perfect the art of unfettered, mindless murder. Granddaddy was going to use her in his larger plan to wipe out his longstanding enemies, regain profitable territory, and eventually reclaim his title as the undisputed kingpin of Chicago. Once Granddaddy finished his lesson, he handed Summer the gold Desert Eagle.

"This is my gift to you. This is your good luck charm. This will help you take over these streets. Shit, over everything your heart desires."

She slowly took the gun out of Granddaddy's hand and rubbed it as if it were her pet. "Thank you, Granddaddy."

"No . . . Thank you." He smiled.

He leaned down and for the first time in his existence, he kissed the young girl on her forehead. She then leaned in and kissed him on his right cheek.

"Now go wash up. I'm gonna get the guys to take care of the rest." Once the "lesson" was officially over, Granddaddy looked at his group of loyal, die-hard henchman.

"Okay, Gentlemen. Let's get rid of these bodies. I got some investors coming here tomorrow!" The men stopped the

conversations they were having with each other and immediately went to work to chop up the body parts into delicate pieces so they could be fed to Granddaddy's den of pit bulls he kept secretly.

Summer went to a small bathroom inside the warehouse and did her best to wash herself clean of the blood and speckles of gut sticking to her body. As she cleaned herself, she stared into the dusty, uncleaned mirror, wanting to continue the rampage. She was addicted to the kill pill.

18

I wanna go outside, in the rain

It may sound crazy

But I wanna go outside, in the rain

'Cause I, I think I'm gonna cry

And I, I don't want you to see me cry

I go outside, in the rain

It may sound crazy

But I wanna go outside in the rain

Once the rain starts falling

On my face

You won't see, a single trace

Of the tears I'm crying

Because of you I'm crying

Don't want you to see me cry

Let me go, let me go, let me go

"I Wanna Go Outside in the Rain" by the Dramatics blared through Granddaddy Luther's car speakers. It was 8:34 p.m., dark and rainy, and faint thunder rumbled in the evening spring skies

as the two took off from the warehouse in Gary and headed back to the Chi. As time passed and the high of vengeful homicide began to wane, deep depression, regret, and guilt blanketed Summer's mind. What in the fuck did she just do? She just massacred three men, men who used to be close and dear to her heart. Although she felt somewhat relieved getting some sort of retaliation for her parents' death, once she quickly sobered up from the drug of retribution she immediately arrived at the bittersweet conclusion that no amount of bloodshed would bring her parents back. She could inflict genocide on the entire South Side and the hundreds of thousands of bodies still wouldn't give her the chance to see her mother's smile or hear her daddy's bubbly laughter again. She looked at Granddaddy and quickly assessed since he bequeathed her some useful tools of death, she was going to without a doubt use them to kill him. She figured out what her Granddaddy Luther was doing. He was playing one big-ass mind game with her, and she quickly determined more than likely her dark villainous elder probably knew all along about Quan's plot to kill her father. And despite him knowing of the plot, he did nothing to stop it from coming to fruition. He had to, since Quan's death would ultimately lead to the easy takeover of profitable turf. How could she even allow herself to stoop so low and become a murderer, she wondered as she continued to drift

off, looking out the passenger window, staring at the thousands of beads of rain slowly dripping down the window. As the melancholic romantic song vibrated in her ears, mentally and emotionally she felt gone. She was dead. Empty on the inside. What was the purpose of even living anymore? she reasoned. Without even asking, she opened the front console and took out Granddaddy's small wooden box of joints. She picked out a fat joint, threw it in her mouth, and sparked it up with a lighter that was also in the box. She took three strong pulls, allowing the weed to take her mind off everything.

Granddaddy looked at her and chuckled. "Damn, girl. You gon pass that?"

She looked at Granddaddy Luther, her eyes now glassy and slightly reddened as the THC moved through her bloodstream. She passed the joint to him. He took his puffs and passed it back to Summer. The two in silence passed the joint back and forth until it was finished. An hour passed. The two arrived back to the Towers. Once inside the apartment, Granddaddy told Summer to head straight to the bathroom, take a hot shower, and change out of her clothes and throw them away in a garbage bag so they could be disposed of properly. Summer quickly marched through the dining room. Her new gift, her gold Desert Eagle, was tucked under her arm for nobody to see.

"Damn, y'all was out late! What in the hell was y'all doin'?" Phyllis barked as she woke up from a cat nap, stood up and made her way to Granddaddy Luther. "I left the chicken in the microwave."

Once Summer got inside her bedroom, she saw Serena sleeping away, looking completely peaceful with her hands clasped together on the side of her face. She leaned down and woke up Serena.

"Shhhhh," Summer whispered once she saw her sister's eyes open and go wide. She could tell her sister was taken aback by her bloodied clothes. "Get up and be very quiet. We are leaving now. Pack your bookbag with some clothes."

"Why? What's going on? Why do you have all of that on your body? What is that? Is that blo—" Serena nervously whispered as her eyes kept trying to register what was on Summer's body and why she looked somewhat disheveled.

"Listen, I'll tell you later," Summer interrupted her sister's constant line of questioning. "Right now, just get dressed. WE ARE LEAVING. We are going back to Mom and Dad, okay?"

"Okay . . ." Serena whispered as she got up and followed her instructions to the T.

Summer quickly left her room and went to the bathroom and turned on the shower. She wanted to give the allusion that she was

167

actually taking a shower per the detailed instructions of her grandfather. She dashed back into the room, dumped out her book bag, and began to quickly pack it with as many clothes as she could stuff. Once she got done, she dashed back to the bathroom and washed her hands and face. Once she turned off the faucet, she then took off her bloody clothes and dumped them in a plastic garbage bag and tied them up. She changed into her new outfit and dashed back into the room. Time was of the essence. Serena was ready to go.

"Stay here, and don't come out until I say so, okay?" Summer whispered.

"Okay . . ." Serena whispered back.

Now for the next plan. Finish her massacre. She started to see red again. She had to in order to get herself amped up. She slowly walked down the hallway and made her way to the kitchen. Body, body, head. Body, body, head. She whispered to herself. This was it. The escape. The liberation she longed for. No longer would she be incarcerated in Granddaddy's dark prison of lies, deceit, and torture. Once out in the living room, Granddaddy was sitting on his recliner smoking a cigarette as usual and sipping on a glass of cognac. Phyllis was dancing to a rerun of Soul Train playing on the TV. Summer looked at the television, taking in the man dancing as he played the guitar. She recognized the singer. It was

Curtis Mayfield: "Freddie's dead. That's what I said. Let the man rap a plan. Said he'd see him ho—"

POW! Summer shot through the television, and it immediately exploded. Phyllis was so taken off guard, she couldn't exactly register what was going on. Summer aimed at her. Phyllis looked at her, "Oh my Go—"

Body. Body. Head. POW! POW! POW! Phyllis's body flew back, and on the final shot, Summer successfully took off half of her head. Granddaddy jumped from his recliner and tried to dash at Summer, but once he heard her cock back the gun and aim at his broad chest, he raised his hands, stood there, and smiled.

"Summer, Summer, Summer . . ." he snickered.

"Make one more move and I'll muthafuckin' kill you. I AM NOT PLAYIN'!" Summer tightened her grip around the gun, and her eyes turned to slits, ready to murder this monster.

"Blood in, blood out. Look at you. You've already changed. You can't go back. This is you now. You're a killer. Embrace it, baby girl. You are a coldhearted, ruthless killer."

POW! "AHHHHH! FUCK! FUCK!" Granddaddy screamed as a bullet exploded into his right shoulder, inches away from his chest.

"I ain't no goddamn killer. You brainwashed me, you fuckin' sick bastard. You kidnapped me and my sister, tortured us, and

now you brainwashed me. YOU'RE A FUCKING MONSTER!"

POW! "AHHHHHH! GOD! FUCK!" Granddaddy screamed once more, but louder as another bullet pierced his other shoulder.

He instantly fell to his knees as he grabbed his bloody wounded shoulders. As Granddaddy reeled in pain, he kept going back and forth between chuckling and crying in pain. His chuckles eventually outdid his cries. As he foamed at the mouth, breathing incredibly hard, he looked at Summer and smiled.

"You're not gonna kill me. I see it in your eyes. You can't bring yourself to do it. DO IT, LIL GIRL! DO IT! HA! YOU CAN'T!"

Summer dashed at him and pointed the gun directly at his head. He didn't say anything as he just grumbled in pain and breathed heavily.

"BOO! HAHAHA!" Granddaddy Luther growled, slightly scaring Summer. She jumped but remained in her place. "See . . . You can't kill me. No matter how hard you try, I'm in you. You're in me. We are the same now. We've always been the same. From the day you were born, you were destined to be just like me. You'll never be able to kill me as much you try . . . after all, like father like daughter . . . You're a daddy's girl," Granddaddy Luther chuckled.

Summer's eyes broadened as wide as stadiums and her

breathing intensified. What the fuck did he mean "like father like daughter"? But she didn't have time for Granddaddy Luther to attempt to play another game of mind fuckery on her.

"SERENA! Let's go!" Summer suddenly aimed the gun at Granddaddy Luther's right knee.

POW! "AHHH! AHHHHHHHHHHHH! FUCK! YOU FUCKED UP MA KNEE!"

"We're gone now. You're right. I'm not gonna kill you. I'll let the wolves in the streets get to you, because they're coming eventually. If you try to find us or track us down, I'll kill you. I'll FUCKING KILL YOU!" Summer viciously growled as she dug the gun into Granddaddy's throat.

She could feel his gulps reverberate through the barrel of the gun. He didn't respond or say anything. He just smiled and laughed like a lunatic. Serena came racing out of the room with her book bag on her back and also carrying Summer's bag looking like she'd seen a thousand ghosts.

"Come on, Sister. Let's get the fuck outta here." Summer grabbed her sister's hand and the two of them raced out of the apartment.

Once in the hallway, the two of them stormed down the hallway. Nausea and panic took over Summer, and her knees began to buckle in fear. She had no idea what she was going to do

next or how she was going to provide immediate shelter and safety for her and her baby sister, but at this point, anything was better than being enslaved to Granddaddy Luther and his insanity. They finally made their way to the elevators and down to the lobby. Loretta was standing off to the side, dancing and off-singing to Anita Baker's "Sweet Love."

"Sweet love, hear me callin' out your name. I feel no shame; I'm in lo—" Loretta suddenly stopped dancing once she saw Summer and Serena dash out of the elevator.

"HEY! It's late! What y'all churren doin' out dis late!"

Summer turned her head and gave the woman a menacing scowl and then returned her attention to the front doors.

Loretta took off running, "UH-UH! WHERE IS Y'ALL GOIN'! AND YOU, SUMMER, I'VE BEEN MEANIN' TO WHOOP YO SASSY AS—"

Click. "BITCH! BACK DA FUCK UP! FUCK IS YO' PROBLEM!"

POW! "AHHHHHHH!" Loretta screamed as she ducked and scrambled to the side of the wall, looking for cover from Summer's shot.

Summer didn't aim the gun at Loretta though. She shot at a light fixture hoping to scare the crack hoe off so she could mind her motherfuckin' business. Once outside the door, Summer

zoomed past an army of dope boys. She didn't pay them any attention and they didn't pay her any back. They were too busy pushin' that dope, transacting with fiends and clucks; their minds stayed on making money and getting some pussy later that night. Once out of the massive gated complex, Summer and Serena ran down the street. Summer didn't know what was going to become of her life now, but she figured if she could survive seeing what she saw over the last two years, she could survive anywhere.

After all, she remembered Big Nate always telling her, "If you can make it in the Chi, you can make it anywhere . . ."

19

11:23 p.m.

Vicious streams of cold rainy air whipped Summer's and Serena's bodies as they aimlessly walked down the dark, empty, shady South Side street. They had been walking now for a good two hours. Summer finally decided her next course of action—call her "mom" and "dad," John and Susan Kaskowitz. Summer didn't want to call the police, let alone her social worker. The last thing she wanted was to get entangled with the foster care system and repeat the same nightmare her and her sister just experienced.

"Summer, I'm scared," Serena cried as she shivered.

Her poor sister was cold and quivering as strong lakefront wind mixed with splashes of faint rain continued to smack them in their innocent brown faces.

"What are we going to do?" Serena then asked.

"I'm 'bout to call Mom and Dad. Don't worry. I am just looking for a pay phone," Summer responded as she tried to fight back screaming and crying.

She had to hold it in for the sake and safety of her younger sister who didn't ask to be put into this horrible, fucked-up situation. After walking for a good fifteen minutes more, Summer's eyes zoomed in to a payphone next to a bus stop.

"There's one, let's go," Summer commanded her sister as the two of them began to run toward the phone.

"Hurry up before someone grabs it!" As the girls got feet away from the pay phone, out of the blue, some random-ass nigga who was sitting inside the bus stop walked up to the pay phone.

"Excuse me, sir, but we got an emergency. We really need to use the pay phone," Summer politely asked.

"Hold on, hold on. This lil cutie just asked me a question. You wanna use the phone?" the man asked, exposing his crooked, yellowish, crusty teeth.

His front tooth had a gold front. He was tall, at least a good seven feet tall, slim, had a Jheri curl, and had dark circles under his beady eyes.

"Yes, we have an emergency. Please!" Summer once again asked, but this time a sense of intense urgency and trepidation was buried in the features of her face, body language, and tone of voice.

The shady nigga snickered, reached in, and rubbed Summer's cheek. "What you willin' to do to use it?" The man licked his lips

and grabbed his visible semi-hard dick protruding from his jeans.

That was it; that was just Summer's cue to end this nigga's fuck shit. Unbeknownst to the pervert, Summer just finished killing four people and now was at the point where she wasn't afraid to kill if need be.

Quickly realizing the game this nigga was playing, she fake smiled, "Anything . . . You can have this young, tight, wet pussy if you let me make that call . . . I'll even suck your big brown dick . . ."

The man instantly fell right into her trap. He hung the phone up and grabbed Summer, and before he could attempt to grind his dick on the young girl—click! The pervert's eyes widened in absolute fear at the sound of Summer cocking her Desert Eagle's hammer and digging the massive gold gun's barrel into the man's stomach. He looked down, and all he could see was light from the bus stop bounce off the gold lethal pole.

"You got five seconds to run down the street and get the fuck away from us. FIVE. FOUR. THREE . . ." Summer barked.

The pervert took off like Carl Lewis in the '88 Olympics, sprinting NOT for the gold but FROM the gold—the dangerous hammer tightly gripped in Summer's murderous hand.

POW! POW! "Oh shit! Dey shootin'!" a distant young male voice echoed, warning others in the area of gunshots.

Summer let off two warning shots, ensuring no one else would come and try to fuck with her and her sister. She slid the gun back into her lower back and went up to the payphone. She searched her book bag for some loose change and found enough money to make a phone call. Once she dialed away, she anxiously waited for John or Susan to pick up on the other line.

Ring. Ring. Ring. Ring. Ring. "Come on, come on, come one, come on," Summer whispered as she searched around the dark surroundings and rapidly tapped her foot against the cracked concrete of the sidewalk.

"Please, please, someone pick up . . ."

"Hello?" John finally answered.

"Dad . . ." Summer shrieked as a tear fell from her eye.

"Who is thi—Summer? What's going on? Why are you calling me?"

"Please, Dad. Luther is crazy. He's a killer. A drug dealer. He's a psycho. Serena and I had to escape! Can you please help us! PLEASE!"

"Oh my God, Summer! Where are you now? Do you feel safe?"

"We're here at a pay phone near this bus stop." Summer looked at the bus stop to see exactly which street she was on. "We're at the #2 King Drive bus stop on 18th Street."

"Okay, Summer, stay RIGHT there! I can't come and get you, but I'm gonna call a taxi to come pick you all up immediately. Please, Summer, STAY RIGHT THERE!"

"Okay, Dad, please hurry," Summer cried. "Thank you. I love you."

"I love you too . . ." John deeply uttered.

Summer hung up the phone. It had not even been a good ten minutes, and just like John said, a yellow taxi cab pulled up to the bus stop. The girls quickly jumped in and the driver took the girls all the way back to the Kaskowitz estate up in the North 'burbs. The yellow cab pulled up to the front gate of the Kaskowitz estate. "How do I get in here?" the smelly African cab driver asked in his deep accent, instantly waking the two girls up from a long, much-needed nap. The second the girls got in the cab, they had drifted off to sleep.

"Sorry . . . I know the code," Summer responded. "It's 24-68-20-10."

Following her instructions, Mamadou (Summer saw his name on the placard posted on the back of the front passenger seat), rolled down his window and quickly entered the code. Seeing her old "home" quickly slapped her into ecstasy. She was back in "heaven." Once the driver drove further through and made his way to the front of the immaculate palace, he parked the car and all

three got out.

"Wow! Dis iz nice! Yo paddents got uhlot eh moni, eh?" Mamadou asked.

Summer barely understood what he was saying. She just nodded her head and muttered "Yeah . . ." Summer and Serena quickly walked up to the front door and rang the doorbell.

Seconds later, John creaked his head out the window and then fully opened the door. "DADDY!" Serena shouted and lunged at John.

Prepared to hug her, he opened his arms wide and gave Serena a huge hug. Summer walked up and gave John a huge hug as well as all three of them cried.

"Oh my God! You guys have grown SO MUCH! Oh my God!" John cried as he continued to hug the girls, rocking them back and forth. "Here, come on in! It's still kinda rainy out there it looks like . . ." He led the girls in.

Mamadou walked up to John and shook his hand.

"Thank you so much. Here's a little extra for the long ride." John handed Mamadou three crispy one-hundred-dollar bills and patted him on his shoulders.

"Tenk yoo suh," Mamadou smiled, exposing a big gap between his big teeth, stuffed the money in his pocket, and walked back to his cab.

After John helped the girls quickly get situated back into their once home, he rummaged through his vast fridge, pulled out a myriad of leftovers cooked earlier that night by the chef, and prepared a quick midnight dinner for the girls, who looked starved and miserable.

"I hope you all enjoy . . ." John smiled as he sat two plates in front of the girls along with a tall glass of raspberry lemonade, Serena's favorite.

All three of them were sitting down at the table. Summer and Serena munched away as if they had not eaten a real, nutritious meal in years. John, who was in his maroon and black checkered silk robe, sat and observed the girls, taking in the visible changes they'd gone through over the years. He noticed Summer was much taller, and although a tad bit underweight, her teenage body was now more developed. She didn't look like the little young, prepubescent Marvel comic book reading girl he once knew. She looked like a young woman. He noticed Serena had also grown tremendously. She had a thick head of curly light brown hair, her eyes were much larger and pronounced, and he could also see her body was quickly going through some slight changes. After making light conversation with the girls, Summer mostly recounted the horror of what her and her sister went through since living with Granddaddy Luther. She went all the way—telling him

everything. The mistreatment of Grandma Hattie Mae Mary. The savage, violent rape and murder of Georgette and Father Flake. Phyllis's unfulfilled welfare fraud machinations. The underground drug operation. And once she got done building her case against the villainous "grandfather" of hers, she confessed to killing the three once close family friends along with Phyllis. John was completely stunned and didn't even know what to say.

"First thing in the morning, we're gonna go straight to the police. It's gonna be alright. I promise. This time, we're gonna fight this and make sure you guys don't end back up in hell. I promise. I love you girls," John reassured as he rubbed their shoulders as they continued to eat.

There was one question lingering in Summer's mind though, once she set foot in the house. Where was "Mom"?

"Oh, Dad, by the way, where's Mom? Is she upstairs sleep? You didn't wake her or tell her what was going on?"

John exhaled. "Well, I wanted to wait until you guys got here and got settled in . . . I don't know how to say this the easiest way, but right after you all left, Susan's cancer came. She was diagnosed with terminal lung cancer and died months later."

"Whhaatt?" Summer cried as tears fell from her eyes.

Maybe this made sense all along as to why John and Susan never came to the girls' rescue, Summer reasoned. The girls

suddenly stopped eating and began to bawl.

"Oh noo, noo, shh, girls, please don't cry. Please. You're gonna make me cry as well," John muttered as he struggled to contain his sobs and tears.

"Is that why you all never came back to get us?" Summer asked.

John shook his head as his eyes got super-watery. "Yes . . . Yes. She didn't want you all to see her pain. It would've been too hard on you all. You all already lost one mother. She didn't want you to lose another."

Summer closed her eyes and lowered her head and shook it. She was instantly brought back to that first night when she awoke from that horrible nightmare and panic attack:

"I just don't know who's gonna love us like they did."

"Awww, Summer. Don't say that," Susan cried.

She lifted the young girl's chin, wiped her face free of tears, looked at her, and smiled. "I'm gonna love you all. I'm gonna try my damn best. That's why we adopted you, because we wanna love you."

"Summer . . ." John said as he rubbed Summer's back, lifted her chin, and wiped her tears from her cheeks. "She loved you all. That was one of the last things she told me to do. She told me if I ever got the chance to see you all again, 'Tell those girls—I'll

always love them.'"

"That means a lot to me, Dad. It really does . . ." Summer muttered as she began to eat again and took a sip from her glass of lemonade.

After the girls got done eating, Summer helped her sister get reacquainted with her bedroom and helped her with showering. Once she got Serena tucked away in bed, they said a little prayer and Serena eventually drifted off to sleep. Summer then made her way to her bedroom, took off her damp clothes, and proceeded to take a long shower. She lathered herself in so much soap and shampoo, doing her best to rid her body of that horrible smell— the disgusting mixture of urine, malt liquor, cigarettes, fried chicken, shit, and fishy pussy reminding her of the hellish nightmare she by the grace of God escaped. Once she got done showering, she slipped into her old bath robe still hanging on the back of the bathroom door. Susan and John never got rid of the massive amounts of clothes they bought for the girls since they were hopeful the girls would soon return. Once inside her room, she slipped into her nightgown and made her way to the huge queen-sized bed. Before she went to sleep though, she didn't tell John about the gun on her, or even the hunter's knife she kept in her book bag. She hid the gun in a shoe box in the closet. She got the knife, lifted the mattress, and tucked the knife away. Then she

got on her plush mattress and slowly drifted off to sleep. She was hopeful more than ever her life would have some sense of normalcy now. But there was just one thing she couldn't let go of: Zayn.

"God . . . please, if you're out there. Please, please. I beg you. Let it not be true. Please let Zayn still be alive. And keep him safe. I love him," Summer whispered and dozed off to sleep.

"Ohhh, bitch, you taste so good, taste like vanilla cupcakes. This pussy is so juicy," Keisha spat as she dug her wide, long tongue in between Summer's untapped vagina.

Summer tried to resist and fight, wondering how in the hell Keisha ended up all the way in Scranton, inside her bedroom. She screamed and fought, but she couldn't move because her hands were tied up to the bed frame.

"Lil girl," Granddaddy growled as he appeared out from the darkness. His eyes were bloodshot red.

He was completely naked. His seventy-year-old dick was black, long, and hard. He slowly stroked it as he sauntered over to the bed, ready to rip into Summer's virgin insides. Out of nowhere, a big vat of Vaseline appeared in his hands. He lathered his dick up as he chuckled, blood spewing from his mouth and gunshot wounds on his shoulders. He got on top of Summer and mounted her.

"I told you—you are in me, I am in you. And I'm ready to get really deep in you. SINCE YOU TRIED TO LEAVE ME!" Granddaddy Luther roared as he opened his mouth, his rotten teeth sharp, like vampire fangs.

He dug his mouth right into Summer's neck.

"AHHHHHHH!" Summer screamed as Granddaddy pierced her neck and ripped through her tiny pink vag.

"HELP! HEEEEEELPP!" GASP!—Summer suddenly woke up out of a nightmare.

Her heart was beating a million beats per minute. Her breathing fast and shallow. She dashed out of bed, stormed into her bathroom, and tried to contain her rapid breathing. She turned on the cold water faucet, filled the sink up to the brim, and dunked her face in, hoping the icy water would kill off the mania. A minute passed and her panic attack waned. What a fucking nightmare, she thought. But one thing she did notice was how heavy and nauseated her entire body was. It was as if she was coming off of an intense body high, a high not even similar to the weed or alcohol she consumed those few times with Granddaddy.

20

The next morning Summer woke up, feeling refreshed but still a bit dazed from her panic attack. That was the first time she had a nightmare with such intensity, rehashing her fucked-up experience with Keisha and the Lady Goons. But the one thing that disturbed her was seeing Granddaddy Luther on top of her, biting her like he was a vampire and then raping her. Granddaddy never did anything like that to her, but she assumed being under Granddaddy Luther's long reign of terror was so traumatic, she was capable of dreaming up anything. After she got up, washed her face, brushed her teeth, and got dressed, she headed downstairs to the kitchen to see if Serena and John were already awake. And lo and behold they were. Ms. Albertina, the chef, was in the kitchen whipping up what smelled like a huge Southern-style breakfast. John was at the dining room table in a T-shirt and a pair of jeans reading the newspaper. Serena was in the living room watching the Disney Channel.

"Good Morning, Dad . . ." Summer announced once she made her way near the dining room.

"Summer!" John looked over his newspaper and smiled. "Sit

down and have some cranberry juice. Did you get some good sleep?"

"Yeah . . . Kinda . . ."

He chuckled. "What do you mean by kind of?"

"Ehhh, I had another nightmare, but it's all good. Wow, it smells good in here." Summer quickly shifted the conversation, sat down, and sipped on a glass of iced cranberry juice.

"Yup, Albertina is making your favorite. I remembered it perfectly! Crème brûlée french toast, scrambled eggs, maple turkey sausage, and bacon!"

"Oh my God! That sounds so good right now. You won't believe what we used to eat for breakfast back at Granddaddy Luther's apartment." Summer sipped again on her cranberry juice.

After the family had breakfast, they sat around and chatted for an hour. "Soooo, Serena, I have a surprise for you. You remember your friend, Rebecca, from school?"

"Yeah!" Serena was splashed with excitement.

Her and Rebecca were besties for over a year. "Her mom is coming by soon so you guys can hang out. It's one big surprise. She doesn't know yet. Her mom wants you all to hang out with each other the rest of the weekend. So go pack up a travel bag quickly! They'll be here in no time!"

"Oh my God! Thank you! Thank you!" Serena lunged out of

her seat, hugged John, and then dashed to her room to go pack her overnight bag.

John turned his attention to Summer. "I figured you and I could spend some time together to really get down to what we need to tell the police. At first I know I said I wanted to go ahead and call them today, but we need to make sure we get your story right. If we don't, we run the risk of you going to prison. I am going to hire a very good criminal defense attorney. His name is Mark Lieberman. The best in Chicago. I went to law school with him."

Summer got super-anxious. She felt as if she was totally innocent. And truth be told, anyone could make a good argument she was. Granddaddy Luther brainwashed her with torture and deception and then cunningly used the trauma of her parents' murder-suicide and her thirst for revenge to get her to kill. And she knew if she didn't kill, she'd be killed. So the idea of going to jail, let alone prison, was scaring the shit out of her.

"Okay . . . I understand. You're right. It's a lot I saw and I don't want to come off as if I willingly participated in his craziness."

"Exactly." John smiled. He got up from his seat, "I'm gonna go help Serena make sure she has everything. Go in my office, and I want you to get out a notepad and a pen and start recollecting

everything from start to finish. Try your best just to state facts. Don't get too emotional or explain how you felt. Just facts and estimations of dates, okay?"

"Okay," Summer said as she got up from the table and walked away. "I'll try my best . . ." After John went upstairs to go help Serena finish packing for her weekend trip, Summer made her way into John's office.

She sauntered over to his red oak desk, pulled out the huge black leather office chair, sat down, and immediately searched the desk cabinets for a legal pad and pen. She opened up the top drawer of one of the desk filing cabinets and saw a small white legal pad and a blue ink pen next to it. Once she lifted up the pad, her eyes immediately focused on the words "Final Divorce Decree and Order" on the center top of a folded-up bundle of papers. She knew she shouldn't be prying. Big Nate always told her to mind her own business, but seeing the word "Divorce" immediately raised red flags in the young teen's mind. She waited a moment, looking around, hoping John wouldn't suddenly bust in and catch her snooping through his shit. The second she felt she was in the clear, she swiftly pulled the paper out and read the entire document. Although it was mostly unintelligible legalese, Summer understood one thing for certain. John and Susan got a divorce a month after she and Serena left. This totally conflicted

with what John told her and Serena last night. Did Susan, or her "mom," really die of cancer? Why did they divorce? Summer had a million questions floating in her scattered brain. She quickly put the paper back into its place, making sure it didn't look like it was moved. Summer spent the next twenty minutes writing down everything that happened during her time with Granddaddy Luther verbatim and attempted doing her best not to inject any type of emotion or superfluous feeling. Just like what John told her to do. She recounted everything—from the initial abuse and the mistreatment of her "grandmother," to the murders, witnessing the drug operation at the secret warehouse, etc. She did her best to paint very vivid, exact details of everything. Ding! Dong! It was the doorbell. Summer, not wanting to interrupt herself from writing, continued as she could hear in the background John chat with Rebecca's mom. Summer also heard the two girls, Serena and Rebecca, shout in excitement at seeing each other for the first time in over a year. After Serena, Rebecca, and her mother left, John coolly made his way into the office.

"How far did you get?" he asked as he approached Summer and walked behind her.

"I'm done actually . . ." Summer nervously responded and handed John the legal pad.

As he still stood behind her, Summer stared off at a picture of

her and Serena on his desk as John stood in silence, scanning every single detail Summer wrote out on the legal pad.

"Wow. Okay. Okay . . . well. This is good. This is very good," John muttered as he slowly rubbed his goatee.

Summer turned in the leather office chair and looked up at John. "Should I write more or do you think I should just leave it at that? I did my best to make it as factual and non-emotional as possible."

"Hrrrm . . . Actually, what I want you to do is this. Give me the pen," John commanded.

Summer handed him the pen. He looked at the legal pad and scribbled a few things. Once he handed the legal pad back to Summer, she noticed at the very end of her notes were two lines with an x and then a date.

"Sign there. This will serve as an affidavit, and I'll be a witness that you told me everything truthfully on this paper." Summer, a tad nervous now, looked at the pad and saw John's signature.

She felt a bit reluctant. "Never sign shit." She heard Big Nate's voice faintly in the back of her head warning her to never sign shit, especially when white folks were involved. But she looked at her "dad" and trusted him.

"Okay," she mumbled as she signed away and handed him the

legal pad.

"Thanks, Summer," John replied.

"Okay, next thing. We're gonna transfer these notes to the computer, okay? Do you know how to type?"

"Yeah . . . I was taking a typing class in school."

"Good! Technology is big nowadays. You gotta make sure you stay on top of it. So many changes going on in the world," John said as he turned Summer around in her seat so she'd be directly facing the computer screen. "Go ahead and turn on the monitor and PC."

Summer, doing as she was told, turned on the computer monitor and reached down and turned on the station next to her right foot. John, still standing behind her, gently massaged her neck and shoulders.

"You seem a bit tense."

"I do?" Summer responded.

Truth be told she was very fucking nervous. All she kept seeing in her mind was "Final Divorce Decree." Was this the right time to ask?

"Yeah . . . Just relax. Everything is gonna be alright."

"Can I ask you a question, Dad?"

"Sure . . ."

"Did you get a di—"—GASP—Summer's eyes widened and

her body quivered as John wrapped his clammy pale left hand around her mouth, gripping her with brutal force, slightly suffocating her.

He used his right hand to run a needle into the side of her neck and quickly injected her with an unknown liquid. Once he emptied the syringe, he pulled the needle out and threw it across the room. Summer swung and kicked all over the place, but John increased his grip around her mouth and now used his other hand to bear hug her in the chair. She cried and screamed at the top of her lungs, but her pleas for help were muzzled by John's chubby sweaty palm. Tears flooded her cheeks. As she tried to kick and punch her way out of John's grasp, her slender brown limbs became too heavy to resist the man's sadistic clutch. She quickly faded to black and closed her eyes. Her body slumped in the chair.

21

"I've been saving it just for you," Summer seductively whispered to John.

"Are you playing with me or is this some sort of ploy? I'm not dumb, Summer," John murmured as he continued to stroke himself.

"Kiss me and you'll find out."

He didn't say anything in response. He just looked at her. She looked back him. Seconds later, he leaned in and closed his eyes. Their tongues intertwined as they french kissed each other with full-on passion. After they stopped kissing, Summer bit her bottom lip.

"My young black pussy is dripping wet now. Touch it and see." Summer moaned and breathed heavily.

"I don't wanna touch it. I wanna go in it," John growled and purred like a stereotypical non-pussy-getting, disgusting lowlife.

"I lied." Summer huffed.

John screwed his face up in confusion. "Lied about what."

"You're right. I'm not a virgin. I've been fucking. Older men. Old niggas with big ole dicks. I fucked this one guy named Jimmy

Dean. His dick was so big, but Goddamn, Daddy . . . I am surprised. I didn't think white guys were hung like you."

"They aren't . . . Jewish boys are though," he snickered and licked his thin cracker lips.

"Question for you though . . . Why did you make me write down everything? That was a part of the plan, huh? Use it against me. I look like a straight-up crazy killer on those pages. You give that to the police and they'll have no other choice but to arrest me."

"Yeah. I figured you wouldn't play nice, so I needed some bargaining chips. You scratch my back, I'll scratch yours."

"So if I fuck you, you're gonna get rid of the papers?"

"Maybe . . ."

"Don't get rid of them. Keep them. So you'll have them as a reminder of what I'm capable of."

"Sexy." John smiled, exposing his wide, slightly yellowish grin.

"I just have one request though . . ." Summer politely asked.

"What's that?"

"First I wanna suck your dick. Can I do that?" she fake begged.

"Say no more." John opened the night stand and whipped out the keys to the handcuffs.

"Oh, I also found this just in case your little nigger noggin tries to get slick," he said as he also pulled out her gold Desert Eagle.

Summer smiled. "It's okay."

He uncuffed her hands but still kept her feet cuffed to the bed. She figured he was going to do that.

"Get on yo' back!" She wanted to now take the command.

"Ohhh, I hear that ghetto girl coming out of your voice. I like!" John got in to the center of the bed, lay on his back, and threw his hands behind his head.

Although he had a slight potbelly, he now had the perfect view to watch the young girl go up and down on his old white cock. Summer spread his legs and began to tickle the insides of his thighs. She'd be damned if she was gonna actually sexually please this man, but in order to accomplish her mission, she had to make a small sacrifice. She grabbed his hard shaft with her right hand and slowly stroked him up and down. She then dug her face into his crotch and sniffed his hairy balls and blew the hair on them. Truth be told, she wanted to throw up her entire breakfast on him, but she had to hold that shit back in order to execute her mission with exact perfection.

"Close your eyes, Daddy. I give some nasty, sloppy, bomb-ass head." At her command, he closed his eyes.

HAWK! She hawked up spit and landed it on his dick. "Oh shit. Oh shit. I should've married a black woman. You all may not be the smartest, but you are the nastiest and the freakiest in bed."

Summer chuckled as she slowly moved her left hand out of the bed and then under the mattress. Once she got a good grip on the hunter's knife, she slowly pulled the knife through the veil of the sheets. Her right hand was the strongest. So she switched hands and gripped his dick with her left. Once she got the handle of the hunter's knife in her right, she blew air on his oozing tip.

"How do that feel?"

"It feels good. It'll feel better if you'll just shut up and stuff that dick down your nigger throat."

"Sorry, massah, I's finne suck dis dick nah!" she joked.

But suddenly her fake smile turned into a blank stare. Her eyes turned to vengeful slits. The walls around her bled red. Her vision was filtered through a dark crimson lens.

"No matter how hard you try, I'm in you. You're in me. We are the same now. We've always been the same. From the day you were born, you were destined to be just like me. You'll never be able to kill me as much you try . . . after all, like father like daughter . . . You're a daddy's girl."

Granddaddy Luther's dark voice echoed in her head and she was once again under his enthralling spell of murder. But this was

no longer just a spell. This was her. Her very primitive nature. A natural born killer waiting to be called out of her. SLIIIIIIIIIIIIIIIIIIIICEE! Summer with perfect precision sliced John's dick right off its base, blood gushing her in the face, splashing all over the bed, forming a huge dark red puddle.

"AHHHH!   AHHHHHHHHHHHHHHHH! AHHHHHHHHHHHHHHH!" John screamed as he attempted to get up, but he was a little too late.

SLICE! SLIIIICE! SLIIIIICE! Summer continued to slice the man up. On his chest. His legs. Arms. Face. Although her ankles were still bound to the end rails of the bed, she got close enough to his neck and dug the tip of the knife into his flesh.

"Please, please, please, Summer. Do-dd-d-don't kill me. I'll give you an-an-anything you want. I have money. Lots of it. Millions. Please!"

"Where's the money?"

"I ha-hhave a safe . . . In the library." She pulled the blade out of his neck and without hesitation tucked it under his left knee.

SLIICE! "AHHHHHHHHHHHHHHHH!"

She sliced right into his leg, immobilizing him if he tried to make a move. Summer looked over at the bed and the blood fleshy remnant of what was once John's hardened cock. She had another idea. Summer luckily had enough reach to grab the keys to the

handcuffs. She unlocked her ankles, got out of the bed, and grabbed the bloody cut-off dick.

"Tell me the combination to the safe."

"25-67-23-45-10."

"Where is it?"

"Behind the 1967 Marvel Comics Edition in the library."

"Open your mouth," she commanded as she dug the tip of the knife into his neck.

John looked at her with fear written in his eyes and slowly opened his mouth. Summer then without a hesitation stuffed the flaccid bloody penis into his mouth.

"Now close it, chew, and swallow." He slowly grinded his teeth on the flesh as blood seeped out of his mouth. "FASTER, I DON'T HAVE ALL DAY!"

He cried as he eventually downed his own penis.

"We can make this quick and easy or we can make this slow and difficult. What do you prefer?"

"What do you mean?"

"I mean . . . how in the fuck do you prefer to die?"

"Summer . . . Pl—" SLICE! SLIIICE!

Summer had enough. Without even giving the pervert time to weigh his options, she sliced his neck, tearing so deeply she almost severed his head off his spine. Summer was a perfectionist, so

seeing John's head not fully cut off bothered her. She dug the knife right back in the massive wound and quickly sawed away until his head was off his neck. She threw his head across the room like a basketball and laughed when it hit the wall.

"Mothafucka," she growled.

The merciless killer walked over to the bathroom and washed her hunter's blade until it was clean and clear of blood and flesh. She then cut the bathroom shower on to super-hot, took her clothes off, and took a long, hot shower, washing her body clean of blood and specks of flesh. Once she got out, she blow-dried and hot combed her hair and then did her makeup. She put on a sports bra, a T-shirt, John's oversized gray Harvard University sweater, some black jeggings and a pair of sneakers she had in the closet. After Summer got done getting dressed, she packed a big suitcase of clothes for herself and Serena. She got the luggage downstairs and then made her way to the library. She snatched the entire row of books off the shelf where supposedly this safe was located. There it was. Summer quickly entered the combination, popped open the safe, and emptied it out. She didn't know exactly how much money it was, but it was enough to get her to where she needed to go. Still in the office, she called for a yellow cab to take her to Rebecca's place so she could pick up Serena. But before she left, she almost forgot one thing. Her "confession." She found the legal

pad, tore out the pages, and stuffed them in her suitcase.

~ ~ ~

"Can you park a little bit further down the street? This family doesn't like cars idling in their driveway. I'll kick you back a lil extra for the troubles," Summer kindly asked the Russian taxi cab driver and slipped him a $20 bill.

"No worries. How long you'll be, ma'am?"

"Not long. Give me about a good ten minutes. I just got some extra business to handle."

"Bounce me another $20 and I'll wait for another thirty."

"Here's $40," Summer said as she slipped the man two $20 bills.

"Trust me. I'll be out in ten . . ."

"No problem!" The taxi cab driver turned up his Russian news radio station.

Summer got out of the taxi cab and made her way to the front door of Serena's friend's house. Ding-dong! Seconds later, Rebecca's mother answered the door.

"Summer! What are you doing here? Where's John? How did you even get here?"

"Oh, I took a cab here. I got super-bored, so I figured I'd hang out with you all."

"Haha! I bet! Well come on in! We're making sugar cookies

and watching movies." Jennifer, Rebecca's mother let Summer through the door.

"Anyone else here besides you all?" Summer politely asked.

"No, it's just three of us . . . well now four!"

"Cool."

Summer pulled the gun from around her back and slammed the handle of the gun into the back of Jennifer's blond head. THUD! "Like father, like daughter . . ." Jennifer fell face flat onto the front entrance. Summer leaned down and pistol whipped her again twice, but this time harder, making sure she rendered Jennifer completely unconscious, if not outright dead. She stood up and looked down at the motionless, innocent woman.

"Sorry . . ." Summer whispered.

Based on the incessant giggles coming from upstairs, Summer knew Rebecca or Serena didn't witness what just happened. Summer took the next two minutes to move Rebecca's body further into the living room and out of sight for Serena to see. She dashed upstairs and to Rebecca's room.

"SUMMER! What are you doing here?" Serena shouted.

Summer didn't look enthused and her face turned flat. "Serena, there's been a change of plans. We gotta go home now. Dad sent a cab to come pick us up. It's a serious emergency."

"What do you mean?"

"SERENA!" Summer shouted.

Serena and Rebecca jumped at the sound of Summer's shout.

"Sorry . . . I didn't mean to scare you, but Serena has to go now, Rebecca. Serena, please go straight to the cab downstairs. Now."

Serena looked at Rebecca and gave her a huge tight hug. She pulled away from Rebecca, grabbed her overnight bag, and made her way toward the door. She turned around and looked at Summer's back and saw the huge gold Desert Eagle tightly gripped in her sister's hands behind her back. Serena's eyes tightened and watered a bit as she tried to fight back tears.

"Maybe I'll see you later, Rebecca . . . Love you, friend." Serena stormed out of the room and then downstairs.

Once Summer heard the front door open and close, Rebecca got up and tried to run out of the room, but Summer stopped her dead in her tracks, shoving her back with one hand in the center of her slim, flat stomach.

"Where's my mom?" Rebecca asked in her unassuming, innocent, white-girl voice.

"She's downstairs still making cookies. I have a question for you though, Rebecca. Does your dad know Serena is here?"

"No. He's out of town on a business trip in Israel . . ." Rebecca flatly responded as she gawked at Summer holding her hands.

Summer's eyes turned to slits. "Anyone else know Serena is here?"

"No . . . We just found out you all were back," Rebecca politely responded.

Summer took a second to respond. She exhaled. "Good."

"Are you about to hurt me?" Rebecca asked.

"No. But I do have another surprise for you though. A gift I got from my grandfather . . ."

"What's that?"

"Close your eyes."

The little white girl closed her eyes.

POW! Rebecca's body flew back once Summer shot the girl in her chest, ripping a huge blood smoky hole in the middle of her pink Power Puff Girls T-shirt. Summer leaned down and checked the girl's pulse. Flat. She then dashed downstairs to the living room. Jennifer was still passed out. Summer hovered over the woman and positioned the gun directly to the back of her head. POW! Blood splattered all over the place as Summer landed a bullet right in the back of Jennifer's head. She tucked the gun in her back and then dashed down the hallway and made her way to a guest bathroom to assess just how much of her victims' blood splashed all over her. Looking in the mirror, Summer noticed she had nothing more than speckles of blood splattered all over her

face and sweater. She ran the hot water faucet and scrubbed her face until it was clear. Then she took the Harvard University sweater off, went back in the living room, and laid it over Jennifer's lifeless body that was now slowly turning blue. She rushed out of the bathroom, down the hallway, arriving at the front door. Before she opened it, she quickly scanned the area making sure she didn't leave any type of critical evidence behind. Nothing. She made her way to the idle yellow taxi cab and got in.

"I told you ten minutes . . . Where am I at?"

"Eight and a half."

Summer looked at the placard on the back of the front passenger seat: Vladimir Gorbachev. "Vladimir . . . I like that name, by the way. We're going to Chicago."

"What part?"

"The South Side . . . Grand Tower Boulevard." Serena slowly turned her head at her sister. Summer looked at her "I'll explain."

22

Knock! Knock! Knock! Summer pounded on Apartment 2210—
Granddaddy Luther's unit. Seconds later, Lil Curtis opened the door. He looked her up and down, giving her a menacing scowl. She didn't say anything in response. She pushed him out of the way and strolled right in with Serena at her side. Once she made her way into the dark, smoky living room, her eyes landed right on Granddaddy Luther. He was sitting down in his brown recliner. Both of his arms were in casts, and his wounded leg was propped up on a table.

"Summer . . ." Granddaddy Luther murmured in his dark, raspy voice.

Summer tapped Serena on her shoulder and pointed down the hallway, telling her to go to the bedroom. "Yes, Granddaddy Luther."

"Sit down . . . Let's talk."

Summer slowly walked deep into the living room and sat on a couch adjacent to Granddaddy Luther. He didn't give her eye contact. He just stared into a new television that was blaring a rerun of Sanford and Son.

"Lil Curtis . . . Light me up a cigarette," Granddaddy commanded.

Seconds later, Lil Curtis sauntered into the living room, whipped out a pack of Newports, and inserted a cigarette into Granddaddy's lips. Lil Curtis lit up the cigarette, and then Granddaddy took two long pulls. He turned his face in the direction of Summer, his eyes now beady slits, and blew smoke into her face.

"You passed the test. I knew all along you had it in you. You got your revenge. You killed Phyllis. You probably killed that cracka. But you didn't kill me." He took another pull from the cigarette.

"Why?" She looked at him.

"I am in you, you are in me. We are one in the same. Like father, like daughter, right?" He chuckled. "You ready to work now?"

She smiled. "Been ready."

"Good . . . We'll start ASAP. Lil Curtis, get my coat. We got some niggas to murk tonight. Time to make this money," Granddaddy barked.

Summer got up from the couch, leaned down, and kissed Granddaddy Luther on his cheek. "I love you, Dad."

"I love you too, baby girl. You're my one and only. Now let's go get a taste of some blood."

Text Good2Go at 31996 to receive new release updates via text message.

To order books, please fill out the order form below:
To order films please go to *www.good2gofilms.com*

Name:_____

Address:_____

City:_____ State:_____ Zip Code:_____

Phone:_____

Email:_____

Method of Payment: Check   VISA   MASTERCARD

Credit Card#:_____

Name as it appears on card:_____

Signature:_____

Item Name	Price	Qty	Amount
48 Hours to Die – Silk White	$14.99		
A Hustler's Dream - Ernest Morris	$14.99		
A Hustler's Dream 2 - Ernest Morris	$14.99		
A Thug's Devotion – J.L.Rose & J.M.McMillon	$14.99		
Black Reign – Ernest Morris	$14.99		
Bloody Mayhem Down South	$14.99		
Business Is Business – Silk White	$14.99		
Business Is Business 2 – Silk White	$14.99		
Business Is Business 3 – Silk White	$14.99		
Childhood Sweethearts – Jacob Spears	$14.99		
Childhood Sweethearts 2 – Jacob Spears	$14.99		
Childhood Sweethearts 3 - Jacob Spears	$14.99		
Childhood Sweethearts 4 - Jacob Spears	$14.99		
Connected To The Plug – Dwan Marquis Williams	$14.99		
Connected To The Plug 2 – Dwan Marquis Williams	$14.99		
Connected To The Plug 3 – Dwan Williams	$14.99		
Deadly Reunion – Ernest Morris	$14.99		
Flipping Numbers – Ernest Morris	$14.99		
Flipping Numbers 2 – Ernest Morris	$14.99		
He Loves Me, He Loves You Not - Mychea	$14.99		
He Loves Me, He Loves You Not 2 - Mychea	$14.99		
He Loves Me, He Loves You Not 3 - Mychea	$14.99		
He Loves Me, He Loves You Not 4 – Mychea	$14.99		

He Loves Me, He Loves You Not 5 – Mychea	$14.99		
Lord of My Land – Jay Morrison	$14.99		
Lost and Turned Out – Ernest Morris	$14.99		
Married To Da Streets – Silk White	$14.99		
M.E.R.C. - Make Every Rep Count Health and Fitness	$14.99		
Money Make Me Cum – Ernest Morris	$14.99		
My Besties – Asia Hill	$14.99		
My Besties 2 – Asia Hill	$14.99		
My Besties 3 – Asia Hill	$14.99		
My Besties 4 – Asia Hill	$14.99		
My Boyfriend's Wife - Mychea	$14.99		
My Boyfriend's Wife 2 – Mychea	$14.99		
My Brothers Envy – J. L. Rose	$14.99		
My Brothers Envy 2 – J. L. Rose	$14.99		
Naughty Housewives – Ernest Morris	$14.99		
Naughty Housewives 2 – Ernest Morris	$14.99		
Naughty Housewives 3 – Ernest Morris	$14.99		
Naughty Housewives 4 – Ernest Morris	$14.99		
Never Be The Same – Silk White	$14.99		
Stranded – Silk White	$14.99		
Slumped – Jason Brent	$14.99		
Someone's Gonna Get It – Mychea	$14.99		
Summer's Dirty Little Secret – Ernest Morris	$14.99		
Supreme & Justice – Ernest Morris	$14.99		
Supreme & Justice 2 – Ernest Morris	$14.99		
Supreme & Justice 3 – Ernest Morris	$14.99		
Tears of a Hustler - Silk White	$14.99		
Tears of a Hustler 2 - Silk White	$14.99		
Tears of a Hustler 3 - Silk White	$14.99		
Tears of a Hustler 4- Silk White	$14.99		
Tears of a Hustler 5 – Silk White	$14.99		
Tears of a Hustler 6 – Silk White	$14.99		
The Panty Ripper - Reality Way	$14.99		

The Panty Ripper 3 – Reality Way	$14.99		
The Solution – Jay Morrison	$14.99		
The Teflon Queen – Silk White	$14.99		
The Teflon Queen 2 – Silk White	$14.99		
The Teflon Queen 3 – Silk White	$14.99		
The Teflon Queen 4 – Silk White	$14.99		
The Teflon Queen 5 – Silk White	$14.99		
The Teflon Queen 6 - Silk White	$14.99		
The Vacation – Silk White	$14.99		
Tied To A Boss - J.L. Rose	$14.99		
Tied To A Boss 2 - J.L. Rose	$14.99		
Tied To A Boss 3 - J.L. Rose	$14.99		
Tied To A Boss 4 - J.L. Rose	$14.99		
Tied To A Boss 5 - J.L. Rose	$14.99		
Time Is Money - Silk White	$14.99		
Two Mask One Heart – Jacob Spears and Trayvon Jackson	$14.99		
Two Mask One Heart 2 – Jacob Spears and Trayvon Jackson	$14.99		
Two Mask One Heart 3 – Jacob Spears and Trayvon Jackson	$14.99		
Wrong Place Wrong Time – Silk White	$14.99		
Young Goonz – Reality Way	$14.99		
Subtotal:			
Tax:			
Shipping (Free) U.S. Media Mail:			
Total:			

Make Checks Payable To:
Good2Go Publishing
7311 W Glass Lane
Laveen, AZ 85339